SICKNESS IN HELL

SICKNESS IN HELL

THE DEATH OF MANKIND

WRITTEN AND EDITED BY
TARL WARWICK
2016

COVER ART BY
ELI FOUSTERIS

SICKNESS IN HELL

DISCLAIMER AND COPYRIGHT

In no way may this work be construed as able to diagnose, treat, cure, or ameliorate any disease, injury, symptom, or condition.

In no way is the author responsible for the actions of the reader. Any and all names in this work are fictional and are in no way meant to represent any person living or dead.

CONTENTS

SICKNESS IN HELL

CONTENTS (cont.)

This work is dedicated first of all to Craig Skipp and John Spector, whose work "The Scream" is a sickening masterpiece and one of the finest books I have ever read.

Secondly to my fans and supporters who have for so long supported my literary work.

Thirdly, to my friend Nikolas, whose gagging reaction to the preliminary 14th chapter of Sickness in Hell led me to continue a work which I at first did not take seriously.

Finally, to my family for putting up with my maniacal laughter while writing this work in the first place.

SICKNESS IN HELL

EPILOGUE

As he dumped another drum into the swamp, Henry could only hope his chemical suit didn't have another leak in it like the last time; some of the stagnating scum water, mixed with waste, had gotten into a hole in his leg no larger than a pin prick- that spot had burned for most of the day and no amount of soap and scrubbing could wash it off. He knows the waste is probably flammable, but lights up a cigarette anyways since the job is so tedious- the company won't even let him bring alcohol with him, even if he's helping them break the law for five hundred bucks a dump. He wishes to himself that the dumps he took every day were that valuable to someone.

It's not that he didn't like nature- he did- but money talks and it's not like anyone ever really gave a damn about the vast gulch outside of Hillcrest to begin with- when you name your town Hillcrest, after all, he surmises, it must be on the top of a rolling hill, and rolling hills tend to have swamps between them unless you're in the Sahara or the Gobi or some other forsaken place.

"Well shit on Mary" he mutters, as he gazes a little deeper into the treeline, still tipping back the barrel and dumping the contents, before hurling the empty drum into a shallow ditch- a couple of the trees some distance away near where he had dumped the last batch had already died-their leaves red and dry, the bark already peeling back like the scabs of a smallpox patient.

SICKNESS IN HELL

The company had sent him and only him to dispose of the waste- probably to decrease the chances of word getting out that a swamp not too far from the edges of the one manufacturing plant left in the godforsaken town was being filled with a radioactive chemical slurry because the state government was too stupid to build a disposal system that didn't involve "pay Uncle Sam his due" or "keep the waste on your property until the barrels rust and the town is inundated with a flood of virulence." At least the pay is pretty good; he quit his day job around the time he realized that he was making almost as much as an unauthorized chemical dumper- even better since he lived in the core of the town and didn't really need to have a car- he sold that crap back to the dealer and bought a scooter, mindful that the payments were cheaper than the dirt of the swamp mired around his feet.

With a faint sizzle the next barrel was cracked open and the slurry dumped into the scummy waters yet again, a little steam rising from its surface to curl upwards into the trees- Henry imagines the trees aren't too happy about breathing the stuff, but he doesn't care- they would have developed tree- gas masks if they really, really didn't want to smell the radioactivity and the foul vapors of acids and sludge.

Because of the time of year the swamp was usually filled with an assortment of colorful mushrooms which grew in the stillness of the mud and scum- behind Hillcrest's Hill itself and choked with trees and sedges, the air here was always still even in a storm and the little fungi, he remembers, ranged from poisonous grizelles to edible

SICKNESS IN HELL

boletes in the past, but now only one species of mushroom appears to have survived the onslaught of poison being dumped for months and months at a time into the rancid black waters around him- an innocuous looking little mushroom; off gray, with a bit of yellow dotting the stalk and a few peppery black bits dotting the cap. He wondered briefly if they were edible but the smell of them warned him away, fearful of vomiting up his guts.

Indeed the little shrooms were now spreading their web-like hyphae up tree roots and across the water itself, probably gobbling up the chemicals. Henry didn't know much about mycology, but he presumed that perhaps the species was part radiotroph and was actually growing more quickly because it was cleaning up some of the beta emitters present in the slurry at high enough concentrations to knock out an elephant.

He dropped his cigarette and with a few profane utterances lit another one, watching as the dropped butt sizzled on the surface of the waste-water, the heat causing a chemical reaction and causing it to bubble and stew like a kettle of liquefied human excrement over a dung-fire. With a shit eating grin, he briefly considered whether exposure to the slurry or his chain smoking would kill him first- he decided to lay down his bets on "cancer sticks" as being perhaps a more direct method of suicide.

Two more barrels were upended and placed in their shallow dirt tombs once empty and the swamp was fairly steaming with radiation rising up in a wafting sheen, making the foggy air glow slightly with a strange energy.

SICKNESS IN HELL

Henry was tired, and ready to go home, and too lazy to remove the hazmat suit as per standard protocol to clean later- sure, they made cheaper suits that were easily replaced when used, but he was too lazy for that too and had just spent a bit more on one that could be relied upon for multiple usages. For a moment he considered removing it and going for a swim just to hasten the end of his own misery but determined that he should postpone such an act until next week, or something like that.

"I'm done for the day, headed home Steve," he spoke into his walkie-talkie, one of the big clunky ones that make the other party sound like a robot with emphysema.

"Next week you'll be dumping regular slurry, no need for a suit" came across from the crackling voice of Steve- this was fine news, after all he was paid the same amount whether the waste was radioactive or not, and not-quite-as-dangerous waste was easier to dump because you didn't have to tip it out so carefully.

He brushed some tree leaves out of his sparse hair, which had fallen onto his head from one or more of the dying swamp trees. "You know, eventually this whole swamp will be dead" he replied, "Don't you think that will look a bit suspicious?"

Steve, on the other end, hesitated for just a millisecond; "nobody cares about the damn swamp, this town is dying off like a weed on the side of a volcano, just dump the damn waste, there's nowhere else to put it."

SICKNESS IN HELL

I. GUT MUSHROOMS

Rancid Steve was at it again. He got that nickname for being gross- all his coworkers agreed on the title in spirit- now he was jogging up and down the hallways because he had too much caffeine in his blood and laughing with the typical cheesy laugh of a loser- the kind of laugh that you can hear without seeing who's laughing, and you can tell they're a pimple-faced moron.

With his curly, bleach-blond hair unwashed for three days the situation is even worse for the two others forced to work with the man- they considered it a form of torture, Mrs. Pillwaff's idea of a joke, or maybe her way of meting out punishment just because she didn't like them very much. Carl and Tom are doing all the work, Rancid Steve is picking his nose and banging against the vending machine because his greasy chocolate bar is stuck inside. Nobody tended the vending machine, and the factory itself was not in much better shape.

Tom daydreams about hanging Steve from the ceiling and beating him like a pinata until his organs liquefy and slosh out through his frequently unwashed pants, but manages to choke back his rage at Steve and at

10

the world as he sits, bored to tears like he does every other day.

The three of them are responsible for the most critical operations of the Hillcrest processing plant; the factory itself started out decades prior as little more than a little rectangular brick shop, where a few machines had cranked out meats and cheeses from opposite ends, all packed up and ready to be eaten. Now, it's a rather larger, more hideous affair- a brutalist monstrosity dreamed up by Mrs. Pillwaffs' father, who had thankfully keeled over before he could scarify the landscape any further. Their most popular product (arguably the only edible one) is Hillcrest Ham- a sort of spam-like packed meat which is only edible because most of the weight is sheer chemicals- a mix of preservatives and salts that render it only questionably deserving of the title "food."

From the control center they're in, they can shut down the entire system- both ends of the factory, they can play around with the electrical systems, the water pressure, the plumbing, literally everything. The system had been installed back when Mr. Pillwaff was still alive, as he'd been an egomaniacial tyrant and insisted that from his former office he should be capable of doing literally anything. Worker morale had suffered as he slipped into dementia and repeatedly questioned the factory over the intercom while switching the electricity off ten times a day for some weeks before his daughter arrived to take command of the situation.

Mrs. Pillwaff herself wasn't much better- a fat,

deranged tyrant much like her father, only perhaps slightly less draconian towards people at least capable of doing what they're told. Her profuse perfume didn't help; it choked the lungs of anyone within shouting distance with its too-sweet scent and made Tom's eyes burn. Carl had once suggested that if she wandered through the actual packing room the scent would rub off on, and contaminate, the hams, due to its virulence, and Tom had readily agreed to this theory.

Pillwaff had a tendency to at least cloister herself in her new offices in the back of the building, away from the workers- this was a mild improvement; nobody cared if she rotated her roast beef arms in circles to all the hits of the seventies while pretending to be sexy. Everyone knew she masturbated constantly back there, drinking and smoking and applying perfume to cover up the corny stench of her unholy nether regions- but at least she didn't slip into madness like her father and bring the entire affair to a halt. She was getting rich too, because the processing facility was literally the only significant industrial firm left in all of Hillcrest.

It had started with the loss of half their factories with a tax raise and NAFTA- corporate conglomerates, now even richer, bought up the brands and moved overseas. With a good quarter of the town unemployed, a lot of people simply took welfare and then commerce failed too, because nobody had the cash to shop in the small local businesses- only a couple of cheap box stores, each one slowly becoming more dilapidated, had really survived, and the corporate masters of these fronts soon moved them as

SICKNESS IN HELL

well.

Without commerce and shopping tourism dried up, and then a few farms went under because of a protracted drought and because the local population couldn't afford fresh crops. It was a rolling disaster that had reduced Hillcrest to little more than a meat processing plant, a one-horse-town broken-teeth-and-incest sheriff's office, an underfunded and dirty library which was physically attached to an increasingly sad little elementary school, and a few hundred homes that were still inhabited. Those locals that weren't on the dole worked in the surrounding towns and villages and had to travel to do so, but at the very least the crime rate was low and it was clean- or so they thought.

Tom and Steve and Carl aren't really paying attention to the intake indicators in front of them (in Steve's case, off to the side as he has a coughing fit and shoves his hand in his pocket to fiddle with himself furtively.) If they were, they might have seen a little blinking yellow light indicating that the pH of the filtered intake water was abnormal, and that a contaminant of some sort had breached the filter- which wouldn't have surprised them even if they were aware of it, since the filter hadn't been changed as far as they knew since the last presidency.

Unfortunately it isn't just a birds' nest on the outer pipe intake that has begun to dissolve after years of disuse this time, like it was the last time they bothered to check the intake and had to send Carl into the swamp to go dredge up around the pipe opening and bag up some debris; they had finally installed a grating system several years before and thought that was a massive advance in filtration technology.

If Pillwaff and her cronies had bothered to let the monitoring staff know what Henry had been up to days before, they might have been a little more vigilant- those mushrooms growing in the slurry-tainted swamp separated from the intake stream by only a few yards of loose dirt had finally made their way to fresher water- which didn't benefit their growth, but didn't stop them either. Some of those spores had gotten into the intake, and the decaying filter screens installed long ago hadn't stopped them so much as they had provided the perfect dirty, greasy substrate for them to take hold inside the water ducts under the plant. The rusted, leaking pipes there weren't helping, and the entire system was, unknown to anyone in the plant, ripe for infestation by fungal colonies.

The situation worsened over the next few minutes as well; the intake system quickly began spawning hyphae and little, almost microscopic bits of mushroom flesh were now circulating freely past the filter, as the happy little fungus growths pushed their feeding receptacles to the other side of the filtration sheets. With no way to monitor the filtered water (for such technology did not exist in their aging plant) those in the monitoring center could only ring Pillwaff hours later when they finally bothered to check the indicator lights and tell her that they should close things down for the afternoon and have someone replace the filter system. Pillwaff wanted to go home and wear bondage gear while watching dwarf porn anyways, to get herself all greasy and sweaty, so she didn't give a shit and switched

SICKNESS IN HELL

everything off herself.

Down in the shipping room annoying Sally had already been told to go home, but decided to be anally retentive as always and commanded the last truck to dock anyways and she'd load it herself. She didn't like unfinished work- her raging obsessive compulsive disorder drove her mad and she wouldn't be able to sleep if the hams weren't packed and shipped before five o'clock sharp. It wasn't hard- years of doing the odd lifting job herself when others weren't willing or present had left her muscles bulging with veins- perhaps she was stronger physically than any of the men in the plant.

She had no idea the batch was tainted with mutated, slightly radioactive fungus- it's not like the people in the monitoring center really communicated with anyone else in the plant- Sally had just assumed that the filters were clogged by a dead muskrat or some other unfortunate animal had drowned and gotten sucked in, its corpse slowly dissolving into sediment as it flattens against their water intake. She didn't know shit about water systems anyways- who cares?

"After all" she mumbles to herself as she slides her hair back across her freckled face, "the hams are heat treated anyways."

She locks up the loading bay, climbs into her anally retentive minivan, and heads home to go drink herself into a stupor.

SICKNESS IN HELL

II. THE GAY DAY OF GERMAINE

"Well shit."

Germaine Woodsworth was used to the occasional vandalism- it's no big thing after all, in such a community- a former middle class neighborhood, with modest, nondescript suburban-style ranch homes, which had been hit by severe economic stress- in the hey-day of Hillcrest eight blocks of land had been quickly developed with such interchangeable but comfortable homes, but now a good quarter of the homes were empty, and while in such a small community, assault, murder, rape, and such things were very rare, the local teens commonly got bored enough or drunk enough to smash a mailbox or paint a swastika on the road.

This time, or so it seems to him, the damage is a bit more extensive. The trees next to his driveway appear to have been meticulously sheared down during the night, leaving leafless skeletons in their place and piles of shriveling twigs and hacked-up branches behind his car, effectively blocking it from leaving the driveway. To add insult to injury someone appears to have taken a crap on the hood of his car, the little black turdlets crumbly and mottled, like a little shit-meteor or something.

He brushed his hair back- once thick and long, now growing slightly more sparse with age, and lit up a cigarette. True, he'd been "trying to quit" for years, but never really took it seriously. He'd be more pissed if it was

SICKNESS IN HELL

a work day but since he's on vacation he doesn't need his car at the moment, opting for a healthy breakfast before he bothers removing the debris.

In a town like Hillcrest, cars aren't necessary- the few stores that remain open are all within easy walking distance of any of the town homes, and the only bus in the area is for the school- and that one constantly breaks down anyways because the bus driver is also the halfassed mechanic. That hardly matters either though, it takes only fifteen minutes at a brisk pace to go from the post office on one end of the "city" and end up at the edge of the woods near the processing plant. In between, a lush scenery filled with empty stores, half-empty stores, and a few apartments that are hit and miss.

With only two restaurants to choose from it's a no brainer; the diner has edible food while the other diner, which is more of a cheap truck stop, sells hockey puck hamburgers and greasy fries and sour, spoiled dairy products, so he naturally chooses the former- helpfully, it's also closer to his part of town. Germaine is also the tallest man in Hillcrest; decades of inbreeding in typical mountain-folk style had reduced much of the population to deformity of one sort or another, but his father had been from Boston, made a fortune selling his bakery chain, and retired in his thirties to this same town, where he had met his hillbilly mother. With both of them dead, the fortune was split three ways, ensuring him a decent, if not lavish, existence. He makes quick time walking to the diner.

At first he vaguely worries that it's closed- the sign

isn't out front as it usually is, but when he sees people inside he enters, realizing they must have thrown the wooden placard in behind the counter because of a threat of rain- he liked rain, and hated the sunshine- it washed away some of the dustiness from the town and afterwards when the sun came back, for a brief half hour or so Hillcrest was clean and looked alive like it had every day just a decade ago.

The overly-friendly waitresses briefly spar over who will serve "the modestly wealthy and tall dude" and a grinning face is soon leering over his menu and asking what he wants. Annoyed by the treatment, Germaine has to hold back a maniacal grin and prevent himself from responding "a fucking fried rat and a side of roasted bull dicks." He opts for the house special- ham, sliced thin and cooked with maple, with some (admittedly good) hash browns and coffee as black as coal. With the power of a good breakfast, he figures he can take the dead brush in his driveway and burn it- maybe, he thinks to himself, he'll pile it around a stake and burn an effigy of the mayor, or maybe he'll wait until next weekend to do so.

The coffee is strong and the hash browns good, but when he bites into the ham he can sense a little bit of something that his taste buds register as "shouldn't be in ham." He mashes the meat around in his mouth and chews it slowly, pondering this great cosmic mystery.

"Waitress, a moment?"

She swings around, probably hoping he'll ask her to

SICKNESS IN HELL

drop her panties and hump his leg, "yes, dear?"

"This ham was cooked with maple, was there anything else added? I taste something else."

The waitress asks her coworker and she just shrugs- nothing more than Germaine expected; a little pack mentality, some collective ignorance for breakfast.

"Sorry dear I don't think so."

With the gates of the great mystery closed to him like an iron vault filled with treasure that a thief vainly pounds with a chunk of rock, he resigns himsself to try a second bite. A few other people appear to have ordered the same thing; one of them, an old farmer-looking dude with overalls and a red cap, doesn't seem to find anything amiss. He's sitting in the corner smashing a double dose of the ham down his gullet like a starving heron gulping down a throat full of thrashing fish. A woman directly to his side at the counter seems to share Germaine's hesitation though, she glances at the waitresses and, after three or four bites, goes back to her pancakes, as if to say "I will look at the remainder of the ham and neglect to eat it."

The stuff is leaving a slight aftertaste and it burns a little bit too. He worries that perhaps he is just allergic to something in the ham, or maybe someone laced it with LSD as a joke; he always hated it when that happened- his college roommate had been a total joker and had gotten his ass beat more than once due to the same.

SICKNESS IN HELL

He got up and made his way to the bathroom-possibly the only clean bathroom in all of Hillcrest, to rinse his mouth in the sink and get a little bit of whiskey in him; he always carried a flask for just such a situation. This helps, to a large degree, but there's still a little bit of bitter, almost metallic aftertaste, with just a hint of something else; "mushroom?" he thinks to himself. Maybe the chef took yesterday's leftover mushroom scraps and disposed of them as a garnish for the ham or something.

He starts to feel slightly sick around this same time, just faintly dizzy and a little bit nauseous. The ham wasn't agreeing with him.

He shoves a finger into his throat in one of the stalls and sprays the toilet with vomit, not even bothering to clean it back up- the sloppy mix of bilge-colored coffee gut water and ham chunks, with just a bit of hash brown slop, drips around the seat and onto the floor, with a little bit of orange tinge too, so that his bile ducts can let him know they care about his intestinal discomfort. His stomach doesn't miss most of the contents, but it does miss the hash browns.

This makes him feel tolerably better, having purged some poison from his insides, and he manages to get back to his seat, gulp down the last few hash browns, and slurp down another cup of coffee. He tips the useless waitress just to hurry up his departure and, as he leaves, notices that the woman which had been sitting to his side at the bar is also looking a little bit green in the face, clutching her stomach as he walks out.

SICKNESS IN HELL

Halfway down the block, however, just as he passes the hair salon, he feels a twinge in his guts that makes him bend forward almost double, clutching his belly in pain. A sudden wave of nausea hits him again and it feels as though his entire body has suddenly been hit with a hot flash, tingles running up and down the entire length of his form, leaving a cold sweat in their wake almost immediately. He fills his pants with shit as well, unable to hold that back. What comes out is an abominable mixture of slime that cakes his thighs and drips down until the world can witness Germaine's loose bowels releasing blasts of anal liquid into his shoes. The embarrassment lasts for only a moment—firstly, because the street is mostly devoid of people anyways, and second, because two other people on the same street are suffering similar problems.

At almost the same time that he lurches to the side and props himself against the brick front of the salon, half a block behind him the same woman from the diner steps out into the street and wails with discomfort, puking her ham and pancakes onto the curb as she stumbles off towards her car, making it about halfway there as she drops to all fours, hit with wave after wave of nausea until there's nothing left and she's just dry heaving. At the other end of the adjacent block, sitting on the curb itself, an old homeless man with a scruffy beard and a knitted cap is filling the same beard with his own horrifying mix. Germaine tries to stand and can't, essentially stuck where he is grappling with dizziness and vomiting again all over himself as he witnesses the soup being released from these two other unfortunate beings.

SICKNESS IN HELL

Whatever was in the ham must have been virulent indeed, for a fourth person soon joins the other three when they have been reduced to nothing more than dry-heaving wretches. A wheelchair-bound dwarf with severe deformities is now wheeling around wildly in the middle of the empty street, making gagging sounds, eventually hitting the curb and falling over sideways, dangling there, strapped into his little motorized dwarf-throne. Thus suspended, he joins them in puking and crying and sweating, and a river of dwarf shit soon joins the rest of the foulness, running from his ass and under the chair, suspending him above a torrent of his own diarrhea.

Suddenly, the homeless man stops wretching and stands up with great haste- staring around with an insane look to him, his face stony, his eyes glaring, as he slowly turns his head around and stares straight at the dwarf shitting in the road. With a monstrous, hideous, phlegmatic yell, he runs at the little man, leaping on top of him with his hands out forward, immediately ripping into the poor, wheelchair-trapped being, pounding him so hard his skull cracks. With a feeble, retarded cry, the dwarf kicks and goes stiff, his brain damaged from the blow, as the homeless bum begins to rip through the wheelchair to get at the dwarf-flesh inside, thrashing and ripping and biting until the lifeless, deformed face is entirely defleshed. Horrified, Germaine watches as the bum rears back, throwing his head to the sky and ripping his flannel shirt off, and he can see the man is... changing.

Little white flecks are appearing on his body, his skin mottled with the veins expanding and apparently

22

leaking underneath his skin, rubbery and discolored like a recently dead corpse. The bum bends down again to eat more flesh, and tosses the wheelchair to the side with incredible strength the moment he has detached the dwarf from this rudimentary cage. The chair itself splits from the motor and goes skidding into a neighboring lawn as super-bum suddenly begins visibly growing deformities right before Germaine's eyes.

Behind him, the woman from the diner has suffered a slightly different fate. Her body has begun to bloat and she gasps for air through a choked, expanding neck, and soon turns pale and blue, literally dying before Germaine's eyes and almost immediately beginning to decay.

With a shriek, the bum staggers back from the dwarf, apparently growing in size at a rapid pace, the little white flecks on his flesh expanding until it looks like the bum has whiskers covering his entire body. Done eating his meal, he once again stands stony-faced, staring behind him at first and then slowly moving his head around until he's facing Germaine dead on. He goes quiet for a moment, Germaine still clutching his guts and trying not to shit or vomit again, and then with a shrieking cry, super-bum launches from his position straight into the air, turning around and giving a war whoop as he begins running straight at Germaine.

III: A LEAK IN THE SYSTEM

Germaine was busy fending off the crazed, apparently sick hobo that was trying to deflesh him, but couldn't stop grinning anyways- what a way to get your life ended, by a hungry homeless man trying to peel back your face and gnaw on your skull. Little did he know the situation was about to go from bad to much, much worse.

He held one forearm in front of him like a shield, bashing the hobo in the face, while shoving him back with the other arm, but waves of nausea were making it no small task- what proper protocol existed for when you vomit, while laying on your back, and no possibility exists for switching to your side to let the spew trickle? Germaine didn't think the bum trying to bite his forearm would react well to such a suggestion- a time out of sorts. Moreover, the bum was visibly decaying right before his eyes and little peels of rapidly graying flesh were flaking off of the man, each one hitting the ground and somehow continuing to move, undulating like little stingrays flapping in some warm oceanic clime, crawling around as if on their own accord.

That's when the ultimate wave of nausea hits him- so hard that Germaine, with near superhuman strength, arches his back and literally shoves the hobo off of him sideways, his skull hitting the pavement with a smacking sound as the flesh there splatters and hangs loosely like the outer layer of a cyst partially removed from its crenelated, oozing core.

SICKNESS IN HELL

He arches again, and at first has no idea what's happening- it isn't nausea, it's something else. Then he gazes at his hands, which he has outstretched, ready to fend off another hobo assault. His skin is changing- what before was slightly discolored from blunt trauma is now turning gray, and the hairs on his arms have begun to shed, replaced with prickly little bristles, not unlike walrus whiskers.

The nausea departs almost immediately while the temporarily distracted bum looks behind him at the much easier prey still gasping and dry heaving down the street- for the woman from the diner is still laying there in a pool of her own discolored diarrhea and vomit. The stench alone, the sour-milk-and-rancidity wafting through the road is more than enough to self-sustain anyone's nausea, sick or not. Now, the nausea he felt before is replaced by a different feeling.

Germaine is starved.

He looks at his arms again and almost wishes to consume them- but they're growing before his eyes and his stomach is contracting. Germaine had never been fat but he'd gained a little cushion for the pushin' over the last half decade or so as his metabolism had gradually waned. Now, his guts look like those of a corpse and his forearms have flattened out like those of a praying mantis, his biceps bulging out with strength he's not used to. Famished, he eyes the distracted bum sideways and gets a subconscious urge to consume.

SICKNESS IN HELL

The very thought is disgusting to him but his stomach and subconscious are double-teaming his brain. With a sorrowful sigh and a grimace he roars in wrath, bringing one fist back and smashing the man who had just tried to eat him in the face, sending his skull again flat against the pavement- following up with two more blows, which bounce his decaying head on the tar like a pumpkin bouncing down a flight of stairs, each time losing a little bit of its shape. With the hobo staggered, Germaine lets out a roar, and is surprised at what comes out- not a human voice, but a sort of grizzly bear howl, as he shoves both of his fists inside the bum and begins to rip out the entrails and guts, throwing them around haphazardly, stopping to guzzle the fluids therein- the bile, the shit, the urine, it all tastes surprisingly good and he can't even fathom why the flavor is registering as "yum."

The bum continues to struggle and attempts to gnaw his forearms again but with his skin apparently hardening into leather and bristles sprouting out wildly like a patch of noxious weeds, the bum's teeth can't penetrate his flesh. With one last blow, he sends the hobo to Hell and continues his feeding frenzy. Around the time the hobo is completely stripped of flesh from the upper chest to the knees, Germaine's hunger subsides again. He feels strangely energized, as though his metabolism has skyrocketed, all of his senses supercharged, an ache in his arms, legs, chest, and shoulders as his muscles continue to fill out, replacing his skinny corpse stomach with layers of tissue, with apparently not an ounce of fat anywhere on him. He wishes he had looked this good years ago, he would have gone into competitive weight lifting.

SICKNESS IN HELL

The sickening sloppage laying in the street is now a foul mix of blood, urine, feces, and scraps of flesh of various types, which he had thrown around in random directions while feeding. Germaine still has no idea what's happening- normal days don't include "almost eaten by crazy bum" or "consume said bum and apparently double in muscle mass in a few minutes." Confused, he scratches his head and a little bit of flesh comes crumbling off- somehow, subconsciously, he gets the hint that he should probably eat it, since eating apparently makes him a super mutant, or something of that ilk. Largely not versed in science fiction, Germaine assumes that he has contracted some sort of virus which has turned him into a sort of high-metabolism cannibal and he half expects (with a twinge of fear) the police to come roaring down the street to put him out of his misery.

The police won't be coming.

While Germaine stands around in the road, watching the diner woman continue to heave out her guts, pondering the nature of exotic viruses and bacteria, the kind folks at the Hillcrest processing plant, the maintenance team, that is, are busy crawling around in the duct works, trying to find the source of contamination in their filtration system. Paid twenty smackeroonies an hour, they're in no hurry. Were Hillcrest not a shitty little town with low safety standards, someone might have gently reminded the three workers sitting lazily in the maintenance tunnel immediately adjacent to the intake pipes that it's "not a good idea" to light up a cigarette when in the presence of potentially explosive or flammable vapors. To the three

SICKNESS IN HELL

interchangeable men eating their salami sandwiches and pretending to work, this advice is meaningless, and the youngest among them, a dropout mentored by the oldest, there's nothing wrong with having a smoke in the tunnels while you scarf down a cheaply made truck stop diner grinder.

With a flick of his lighter this particular headstrong novice plumber manages to immolate the entire crew. At first, a slight wisp of flame wafts from the lighter itself through the air, whirling and twirling for a few seconds, dancing slowly along a vapor leak to the pipe system, filled as it were, unknown to them, by spores and hydrogen gas, and the eldest worker sees this and screams in terror as he tries to get up, hurling his sandwich towards the vapor flame, searing a slice of salami in the process, which lands with a smack on the piping. He manages to run up the tunnel for about a half dozen steps before the fire hits the pipe and sizzles inside for just a moment before the entire pipe explodes with the force of a bunker buster, and in a flash of flaming hydrogen, the entire bottom level of the plant is engulfed.

The fireball rises from this basement sub-level through the packing plant itself on a cloud of flaming spores and burns hot enough to sterilize them all, but not hot enough to sterilize the little chunks of radioactive fungal flesh whirling around the hellstorm. Little bits of processing plant are fired out in every direction for a quarter mile- easily encompassing a large proportion of the low rent part of Hillcrest, showering it with flaming debris, igniting homes and smashing cars with bricks and cinders.

SICKNESS IN HELL

The small mushroom cloud rising from the plant contains a large number of mushrooms itself; little bits of mushroom flesh, toxic, radioactive, and infectious, are thus scattered in partially vaporized form all over the town, the hazardous fumes furling out from the burning sub-level like a wall of fog rolling into London on an average day, the poisoned mist working its way down street after street, filling the entire area with sickness. The choking, off-fungus scented breeze reaches Germaine and rolls on past, continuing down the avenues and roads until they hit the next line of hills, which funnels them down the hill of Hillcrest itself, dissipating around the farms and rural cabins down below some hundred feet or so in elevation.

Unknown to any onlooker the radiation level has also risen substantially- the sub-level is not far from the terminal point of the intake, and the intake is only a few yards from the swamp where Henry had been depositing poorly treated, poorly sealed drums of chemical slurry. That the local nuclear plant had been in collusion with the processing plant itself and agreed upon dumping their collective waste together made the situation even more hazardous- the air around Hillcrest, as far as the edge of the swamp all the way down around to almost the edge of the next county, was now engulfed with chemical smog, moderately-dangerous levels of beta emitters, and worst of all, the fungal equivalent of a biological weapon of mass destruction.

The rumbling of the explosion and the windy sound of foul vapor rushing past like a small hurricane passes after about thirty seconds- that's all it takes for the relatively compact town to be completely washed in pestilence. All goes silent save for a few people in the street muttering about "what the hell happened?" The explosion has even distracted them from the fact that a visibly mutated Germaine is standing there dripping with hobo blood and poised not two yards from a half eaten cadaver. Under any other circumstances, even the dimwitted, inbred locals would have noticed something amiss from that spectacle.

The vapor quickly begins working- the infection is much more easily absorbed through the lungs than through the guts, as infections tend to be. As though they had been hit with nerve gas, the residents of Hillcrest soon drop in agony as their innards begin to churn and burn, their flesh sizzling with the slurry vapor, their eyes burning, watery, and growing dim from the choking chemical fog.

The noxious nature of the breeze doesn't bother Germaine, nor does it seem to affect the diner woman behind him- possibly because she has already keeled over and stopped jerking around spasmodically to die in a pool of her own bodily waste. Germaine has reason to be nervous though, because although the gas has killed her and two of the other people on the street, it seems not to have killed a half dozen people who come wandering into the street from their homes, jerking around and drooling through the bitter, metallic radioactively-flavored mist. A few murderous shrieks tell Germaine it's probably time to flee from the scene, and he does, running almost on all fours down the side street and working his way back around to his home.

SICKNESS IN HELL

Once there he realizes he should check up on his sister- was she alive? Maybe she's hideously mutated like him, maybe she keeled over or was keeling over actively. He grabs his cellphone and dials the number but the explosion apparently knocked out the cell tower, because he's getting less than a bar of service and the call fails to connect.

The power is also acting up- the explosion must have addled the lines or something, because the lights are spitting and flickering and the microwave is beeping at him to reset it. Annoyed, he hurls it across the room and smashes it.

With no way of knowing whether his one local relation is alright, and with at least one friend unaccounted for, and with distant murder-howls sounding off every few minutes courtesy of an apparent horde of zombies (or so he takes them for) Germaine is faced with the question of what to do next- sure, he technically murdered someone this morning, but that same person had tried to murder him so he figures that about evens it out. He ends up removing his shoes altogether because his feet have grown several sizes and have begun to get discolored inside them- a little greasiness has gathered on their surfaces from the compression, making it look like he grew some sweat glands on his ankles and soles.

He looks out the window and chews his lip nervously until he can almost detach and swallow it.

SICKNESS IN HELL

IV. EPIDEMIC

It didn't take more than a half hour before things went from strange and bad to stranger and far worse. Germaine was largely unawares of what had happened, other than to himself and the bum he had eaten; his body was still changing rapidly, and his muscle mass had continued to grow for some time until it had flattened and fleshed out his forearms and calves until they resembled those of a bodybuilder. While this normally would have been a welcome increase in his overall attractiveness, along with the increased musculature came an increase in paleness until his skin looked like a dead chicken, pockmarked with little bumps and bristly hairs. For a while, the occult-minded Germaine worried that he had been stricken with a curse and contracted lycanthropy. "That's nonsense" he said to himself, rationalizing the whole ordeal. It still didn't make sense that the man he'd cannibalized tasted good to him either, to the point at which he almost wished he had hauled the cadaver into his home.

Outside, the dust of the explosion was still stubbornly hanging in the air and the power was still spotty at best- a brownout of sorts, where a few lights were still dimly glowing. Thankfully, since it was only noon, it hardly mattered. The soot was building up on cars and lawns outside, casting them in a grayish veil of dust, which was also wafting its way lazily in through every crack and crevice of his home, leaving little coke-line looking off-gray layers of grimy stain on his partially opened windows. The heat outside was just enough that he wasn't going to

32

bother closing them.

After a few minutes more he decided he had a
responsibility to check on his sister regardless of the
howling outside from in the distance; he estimated that the
wandering, shuffling beings out there (which, in occasional
passes by his window, still more or less resembled human
beings) were now three blocks off to the left and down a
street; no worries, his sister lived in the other direction
entirely.

With a furtive glance to each side and grabbing the
baseball bat next to his door, he made his way across the
lawn and half-huddled through the street, passing by a
couple of dead bodies on the way. Bloated and already
coated with flies, they must have keeled over in the
suffocating dust because they didn't seem to have been
predated upon to any substantial degree. Sure, one of them
was missing a chunk of hand, but that wasn't the most
lethal of wounds one could receive. A little dribble of blood
had already dried below the wound and had apparently run
a half foot down towards the sewer grating before being dry
enough to stall out, failing to flood the surely rat infested
underworks below.

Ignoring the street, he made his way more quickly
to his sisters' home, through side yards and driveways- over
one fence he went, losing a chunk of loose vestigial flesh in
the process which, unknown to him, had been growing on
his left lower leg- the tumorous clump of vestigiality
merely got tugged at by the fence, and came off almost
seamlessly, leaving behind no wound at all and sitting there

SICKNESS IN HELL

oozing on the grass like a slug basking in the afternoon sun.

Next to his sister's home at last, he hears a cackle behind him and turns, seeing a horrifically disfigured old lady stuck halfway out of her home, gobbling on her dentures and losing them on the concrete in front of her, drooling a saliva-blood mix without the benefit of saying anything coherent about her condition nor anything else. Germaine looks around her and sees her sorry state- her legs had bloated up to such a size that they were crammed into the door frame and she was propped up there, her upper body halfway normal, holding herself up on a walker while her fat, rubbery legs hung there suspended a few inches off the floor behind her. That the woman, trapped as she was, was making him crave more cannibalism, momentarily disturbed him, and he passed up the offer, with more important things, perhaps, in mind.

He knocked at his little sisters' door; at first no answer, and he worried that she was probably a corpse and laying in her bed dead as a doornail, being eaten by maggots. Soon though, a faint shuffling inside was followed by a more or less familiar face gazing out of the picture window from behind the drapes, and then the door clicked and opened. Much to Germaine's glee, it seemed his sister had been fucked up by the "whatever the hell just happened" situation, and between her face being half melted off to the bone and her having grown a long, catlike tail, he was happy that at least he wouldn't be judged for his bizarre physical condition.

Neither of them spoke for a moment and then they

attempted to talk over one another, until his sister had the good sense to push him inside and lock the door behind her. She could recognize him just as he could his sister, even though both of them shared a grotesque level of deformity. Between the two of them there wasn't enough melanin to produce an albino, and Germaine was apprehensive about telling her that he'd eaten a street bum earlier.

"I have no idea what happened" his sister said to him, "I heard a bang and then I felt like I was being choked. I woke up and I looked like this."

Germaine told her his story, minus the eating of the bum, but had to tell her anyways when asked why "his clothes were literally coated in bile and blood." She got bored with his overly long explanation and waved him off on the subject, much to the relief of the slightly worried Germaine.

"I think I'm going crazy too."

His sister's utterance seemed almost normal in the circumstances, but he had to ask what she meant. "I mean," she continued, "that earlier I wished that I had a tail to go along with the rest of this shit, and one almost immediately began sprouting out of my pants like a cobra."

Even in the context of an explosive miasmus killing their entire town and leaving everyone deformed this seemed like a revelation of sorts. "That's impossible." He replied, hoping she'd drop the issue, but he knew she'd stick with it- she tended to obsess over such things.

SICKNESS IN HELL

In the past Germaine had worried that his sister had delusions or schizophrenia, because of her fixation on tarot readings and TV psychics that she claimed had at least several times predicted her future properly. For only 1.99 a minute they diagnosed her entire fate and she seemed satisfied with their predictions, despite Germaine, in those days, chuckling and telling her that he predicted the tooth fairy was going to bash the teeth right out of her lower jaw leaving her unable to eat so much as a cracker.

She didn't relent, predictably, and continued on a diatribe while Germaine stared at her partly awestruck; the street had several corpses in it, both of them were riddled with apparent disfigurements, and she was worried about the one appendage he'd seen today that actually functioned properly. She probably wouldn't have even recognized him if his face hadn't stayed roughly identical to what it had been the last time he got out of bed, save for it thinning out in general until his cheek bones jutted out like crags from some high Asiatic peak.

"Well I wish I had a couple of spines on my hands so I could call myself Mr. Spiny and rip people open with them when they displease me" he replied in sarcastic retort. Then he waved his hands around a bit, chuckling, forgetting, almost, that whatever had happened earlier might be Armageddon or something for all he knew. In a few seconds, though, he wasn't chuckling, he was staring at his hands while his sister insulted him generically and launched into a lecture about how she was always right and people ought to take her seriously.

SICKNESS IN HELL

There, around the bottom knuckle of the index and ring fingers on each of his hands, little bumps were forming, and he suddenly felt a pain in his stomach like he hadn't eaten in weeks, as the skin prolapsed, bled, and sealed itself back off around four short studs growing right out of his bulging knuckles, until he was left with four extremely sharp spines, two on each hand, each one about two inches in length. With such surprise he didn't even react when his sister called him "lurch" (a nickname he had always hated, due to his height and awkward gait.)

Germaine wondered if it was possible to replicate this act without wishing out loud. "It's not like some magic genie is behind this." He muttered, although his sister was now ignoring his presence and was apparently fixated on being hungry- he almost fell over when she leaped out into the kitchen, threw back the refrigerator door, and began piling into anything she could get her hands on.

"Hey, experiment time sis!" He waved her down from behind the doorway but to no avail- with a mouth full of eggs, shell and all, she was in no condition to 'do some science.'

He mentally focused for a moment, and then mentally 'willed' his body to change- he had in mind something simple, "I want to be a few inches taller" he said to himself, within his own mind. His body obeyed, and he felt the same reeling pain in his stomach as energy or mass or *something* began to drain away like the collective wallets of a city funding the construction of a bridge.

37

SICKNESS IN HELL

With a grin he realized that he should be able to change virtually any physical trait in the same manner. There seemed to be a minor flaw with the idea, though, since each time he altered his body he was wracked with increasing pain in his intestines. First he increased his height, then added a little bit of length to his fingers, then jettisoned those annoying bristles all over his body that made him look like a Hollywood werewolf- much improved, he almost collapsed from the intense pain running from his guts to his limbs and back in a circular manner, like the cycling of some extreme energy there. Where the bristles had once been, now there were empty craters, grimy and off-brown, where the bloated roots of the same had once stuck into his flesh. He might have thought to remove them but thought better.

Sated, his sister returned. "You know, you don't have to wish out loud- I think we're mutated or something" he said, and she, always a quick learner, was soon altering her own body herself- to his horror, though, she decided to fixate on her tits and ass until they were transformed into disgusting, blubbery bags drooping down like sacks of turkey fat from her body. It took her several attempts to tighten the flesh up around them enough to get them to stop dangling down so far that they nearly flapped in the breeze out of her shirt entirely.

For a moment he thought something might be amiss- he was having a brain fart and thought there was some sort of intelligent revelation he was supposed to grasp but wasn't quite fully aware of. Then it struck him; his sister didn't seem to be in pain at all despite overhauling her physical characteristics to a far more draconian degree.

He scratched his chin for just a moment and then looked at his sister like a mad scientist discovering some previously unknown and virulent strain of weaponized parasitic beetle. She appeared to know what he did before he even said it- it only made sense, in retrospect, he believed; in order to change the form of matter energy must be supplied, and mortal beings got energy from food.

Germaine was simply too hungry to be doing that shit at the moment. All he'd eaten was a few bites of infected ham and half of a dead street bum. In addition to normal metabolic processes, a person has to eat many tens of thousands of calories to grow so much as a centimeter- he'd just grown two inches in a few minutes, no wonder his stomach felt so empty. With a ragged shout he piled past his sister into the kitchen and began ripping open packages, dumping anything available into his deformed gullet, choking back his utter contempt for mankind as he choked down his food- cereal bars, frozen berries, raw chicken, milk gone slightly sour, it all poured into his waiting maw until he felt absolutely bloated- he noted that this didn't just do away with his intestinal pains, it made him feel as though he was more awake, alert, and aware- quite the opposite of the result a "normal" human attains from a large meal, where they end up passing out in an armchair listening to polka music and crying about the good old days.

Unconcerned with ethics, it was still surprising how little his morning cannibalism has bothered him, his sister was not entirely receptive to philosophical discussions though, she was busy staring at her tits again, not even apparently caring that her brother was two yards away from her and redesigning his hair, making it grow out thicker, something his premature balding had previously denied him. Germaine wasn't a fan of enormous knockers but did admit his sister looked pretty good without a shirt on. Maybe he'd commit incest later, maybe not, he wasn't sure yet since it seemed law and order was more or less vestigial at the moment.

Both of them perceived a slight scratching noise coming from the front door and jerked around almost in tandem. His sister ended up grabbing the bat and he fiddled around for a moment before withdrawing a knife from the cabinet immediately next to him- under any other circumstance he'd wonder why his sister was keeping the knives in the living room elevated above the sofa but didn't care as the scratching continued. Convinced it was probably just a dog Germaine slowly made his way to the picture window and glanced sideways towards the door to see what being was disturbing the peace, but as he pulled back the drapes, a hideous figure suddenly appeared in the window, startling him such that he reeled over backwards.

There, waving his arms like a maniac and laughing with sadistic delight, was a priest- or what had been a priest at some point in the recent past- a being deformed almost beyond comprehension, a withering corpse riddled with tumors and splotches of decay where the flesh had begun to sag and pull away from arterial connection. Pressing up against the window, the priest, with a shit eating grin, left several patches of loose flesh stuck to it, utterly smearing the glass and turning around to the street. Throwing back his head, he let out another, even higher-pitched laugh, and waved his arms around again like a demented wizard, before turning back to the window, taking a few steps back, and hurling himself against it, shattering the glass as he flailed around randomly, strewing the shards around and slicing much of his own epidermis off in the process. Wriggling down the side of the couch, the priest didn't even bother to stand back up, but began making gobbling sounds, grabbing a shard (and cutting deep into his hand in the process, emitting a spray of arterial blood onto the carpet) and holding it up in front of him, shuffling on all fours towards Germaine apparently intending to slice him up the leg and eat him.

He didn't get more than two half-shuffles before his sister brought the bat down on his skull and utterly collapsed it. The mutated priest jerked around but refused to die, rearing back and laughing again, his rows of teeth jutting out at odd angles from bloated, red gums, bleeding with glass shard damage and decay, a few of the teeth having loosened up and fallen out at some time fairly recently- for a few of them were gone entirely and had been replaced by little bumps and valleys where the nerve roots hung out like little black hairs where teeth used to be anchored.

She pounded him again, this time uplifting the bat right into his jaw, knocking him almost up into the air, sending him back against the couch. The priest was regenerating his injured tissue at a fairly decent clip and

SICKNESS IN HELL

Germaine didn't want to wait all day, so while the priest was down he slashed him across the eyes with the knife, drawing the blade down across the left and back up in a swirl on the right. With his sagging eyeballs leaking fluid and slashed in half, the blind priest became frustrated, and out of the top of his head a new set of eyeballs formed itself as he writhed in pain on the floor- a couple of eye stalks, just like the kind a slug has, emerging like two slimy ping pong balls encased in a membrane from his forehead, spinning around and whirling in circles as his mind attempted to comprehend the new, confusing optic input.

The insane interloper found a chunk of meat loaf on the floor and dove for it, distracted entirely from his quest to eat Germaine's legs like a starving doberman, and left behind a sheet of flesh and blood trailing behind him as he chowed down, laughing again like a lunatic. Two more good poundings with the bat destroyed his head entirely and left him wriggling on the floor like a seizure patient. Germaine chuckled and sliced the destroyed head off entirely, hurling it back out the window, where it remained alive for a few minutes, trying to laugh and shout without the benefit of lungs, blinking and rolling its slug eyes around in circles, before finally going silent altogether and immediately beginning to melt into the lawn. Every blade of grass thus infected with this foul mix quickly deformed as well- there was a yard-wide patch of grass only minutes later that was curled up and mottled like it had contracted some sort of cancer than only infects grasses.

This body didn't appeal to Germaine as much as the bum had- the priest was far more hideous. Little bags of fatty tissue hung from his calves but the rest of him was just skin and bones.

"We should go check the church, if that weirdo got this fucked up there are probably some mutated altar boys or something running around in the church yard." His sister opined, prodding the dead cadaver with the bat, smooshing it through his oily flesh and into the guts, releasing a little torrent of liquefied feces.

It took her a while to convince Germaine- he said that he'd rather go into the forest and see what had happened to the processing plant- which he took to be the almost certain source of the explosion which had occurred earlier.

"Oh come on, we can do that too, let's go burn a church to the ground. I have plenty of fuel."

When she put it that way he was more receptive- church arson sounded pretty damn fun, especially when they might get to see some flaming priests and altar boys stumble from the wreckage burning and screeching in mutated pain. He reminded her that with the power spotty at best they had better return before nightfall to fortify a bit and probably block the stairs and sleep in the second story. She agreed- they'd quickly burn the church and then check the factory, probably eating dinner in the streets since there seemed to be quite a lot of good food lying dead there, baking in the sun and spawning maggots.

V: CITIES ABLAZE

The only church in the entire town was an old affair, riddled with little bits of half dead ivy on one side, flush with thriving ivy on two of the others; an enormous marble building which had gone up almost in the wee hours of the birth of Hillcrest as a community well over a century ago, when it had been a sort of trading hub for local farms and woodlots. Fed a continuous supply of tithes from the pious Catholics which had begun to settle there, the church was splendid in its heyday and even though it was now a bit dilapidated, it was still stately when compared to the atomic era row housing and glorified ranch homes (trailers on foundations, more like) which had been erected during its post-Eisenhower second boom time.

The lot next to the church had been abandoned years before and the decaying home that once stood there was little more than a dry pile of kindling perfect for making a celebratory blasphemy-arson. The church was almost too pretty to burn, but lord knew what mutated freaks might be holed up inside. For years rumors had swirled that the bishop, whose residence was built onto the church itself, was a homosexual and had hired more than one transvestite to strip for him and let him lick whipped cream off his nipples on the altar, but those were just rumors and meaningless in the present context.

Germaine and his sister had hurried their way through back lots to the church to avoid detection from any other fucked up people (or animals, as Germaine worried more about) and it was barely 2PM when they arrived, laden down with four cans of gas and a backpack full of kindling. Neither of them had realized that the lot next to the church was full of available wood and that they had carried this burden for no purpose at all. Germaine quickly began piling wood up against the front side of the church, intending to release a wall of fire that would eventually work its way inside, before his sister stopped him and looked at him like he was a retarded orangutan.

"Yes, let's start the blaze outside so that every freak in the county can see what we're doing. It would be such a stupid idea to start it inside then take shelter somewhere else to watch the festivities, safe from being attacked and potentially eaten." She rolled her eyes. Germaine saw that her suggestion made sense and he chastised himself for his haste.

It didn't take long to get inside. The main door was locked shut- perhaps the priest they had battered and destroyed earlier had been out for breakfast and shut the church up behind him. Most of the windows in the church itself were high up above ground level, the inside of the church being itself raised a yard, with another yard and a half of wall before the bottom of each window began. Rather than waste time smashing a window (a noisy affair) and climbing inside, maybe being accosted by more priests or altar boys or nuns inside, they determined that it was easier to get in through the bishop's offices in the back of the church.

The rear windows of these offices immediately

faced the church yard- an old grave site which stopped being used around the 1970s when the church opened up a new burial ground on the other side of town. The graves here were mostly crumbly and covered in moss- the priests had maintained it in some degree of stateliness until the neighbors told them that the twisted old branches of willow and uneven ground, coupled with the moss and dead leaves, looked more "graveyard-ish" and had a better overall look to it. Reluctantly, they had ceased their endless stream of lawn mowers and weed whackers and let the area go more or less fallow, adding to the local décor. Indeed, in a state of disuse it looked far better.

The windows on the offices were only a yard from the ground, this addition having been built in more pragmatic than idealistic times- it was simple to jam a thin slice of grave-rock into the sill and work the frame loose, allowing them to climb inside once the window was literally ripped off of the wall itself.

Almost immediately they realized that someone had been there recently and perhaps still was- papers were strewn about the office and books once held on the oaken shelves in the adjacent study were thrown about as though a hurricane had swept through and made its way through the hall, where a few more books lay scattered about the dying body of a potted plant which had been rudely upended, the soil cast onto the formerly immaculate red carpet.

With the front door locked and a lack of broken windows they assumed they were not alone and Germaine requisitioned a ceremonial saber from the wall of the office, which was still untouched, while lil' sister prepared to immolate any oncoming attackers with a souped up weed wand. She had always been one to fiddle around with potentially dangerous technology and make it more dangerous than formerly it was- this specific object could be hand-pumped from a can of gas and lit up like a flamethrower. The only drawback was its lack of a stanching method- for once it was started up it had to be continually pumped, lest the flames enter the can and explode it in the face of the user.

"Maybe you should use your baseball bat, it's probably safer, we're indoors you know."

"We're here to burn things anyways, my silly brother" she told him.

"If that can goes off I don't think being hideously mutated will be much help; you'll scorch yourself into a pile of ashes and me along with you, now p-"

He stopped when he heard a thumping noise from the hallway outside of the office- it sounded like something limp and heavy being dragged.

His sister was ahead of him in reacting and immediately took up a spot beside the door, so that should it open, she would be behind it, readying herself with a meat cleaver and crouching slightly, ready to slam it into the head of anything coming through. With a saber in his hand Germaine felt just fine- in a total "shit has hit the fan and begun to spray all over my face" scenario, he figured they could both just bolt for the torn-off window anyways.

A gurgling sound then sounded from behind the door, like a gallon of sticky phlegm being circulated through an artificial lung. A tapping on the door reminded them they weren't alone, but no apparent attempt was being made to open it, so Germaine motioned for his sister to take up arms on the other side of the door, and he'd open it.

Cautiously, he reached out for the knob, trying to turn it as silently as possible, before flinging it back- and although what was behind the door startled him, it seemed the being there was even more frightened.

With a yelp, the hideous man on the other side, mottled from head to toe and fleshed out like a gigantic pile of blubber, tapered up to his hairline like a conehead, fell backwards and waved his arms frantically, losing his balance and slamming to the floor. With a cry of fear he rolled onto his side with his arms clasped in agonizing terror and began babbling and pleading not to be killed.

"I didn't do anything! I'm not a monster! Oh lord why did you curse me!?" He was literally crying at this stage, and Germaine, who had partly fallen back from the door in startled awe, pulled himself forward on the frame and stared down at this vaguely dwarf-like wretch, who was almost bowing before him. His sister moved around the door, and the man looked up and continued.

"Please! Beautiful girl don't kill me, Please!"

SICKNESS IN HELL

"Who the fuck are you?" Lil' sis was almost smirking- they had been worried some pile of muscle was on the other side of the door with a war hammer or something like that, but here was a man shorter than her, older than Germaine by at least three decades, and almost unable to move. She reckoned the thumping sound had been his legs, for hardened nodes of leathery flesh, brown in color, were poking out from his enormous pants, thumping the floor like little bits of tree bark every time he moved his legs.

"You're not going to hurt me? Oh thank you please, I've already been chased twice today. I locked myself in the closet..."

"I asked who you were not for your life story." She didn't like religion, she didn't like religious people. She was hoping he'd dispense with the blubbering and give them a name.

"I'm Adam, I was here to clean the floors, I'm the janitor, but then the priest went mad and began chasing me, I had to lock myself in the closet and he left, cackling like Satan the whole time."

At last they knew roughly what was happening; the poor janitor had been accosted, probably by the same priest they liquidated earlier. "Well the priest won't be coming around anymore, we bashed his brains into his neck earlier when he tried to eat us." The little man stopped crying almost instantly and a look of profound joy crossed his face.

49

SICKNESS IN HELL

"He's dead?"

Germaine and Lil' Sis nodded. The man sighed like a cancer patient told they were finally in remission after years of chemotherapy.

"Can I come with you? I'm not even from this town, I have no clue what's going on."

Germaine questioned him about the explosion earlier. "Did you see where it came from? Was it the processing plant or somewhere else? It looked like it came from there."

"Yes, I was literally cleaning the bell tower when it happened. I almost fell off the side onto the roof- the plant has been wrecked. It's been a disastrous day all around. When the smoke coming off the plant hit me, all I could taste was bitterness, like hot iron on my taste buds, then I passed out and when I woke up I was covered in sores, and then the priest chased me when I went back down to the offices to tell him what was happening, so I locked myself in a closet, and a while ago, when I came out and went into the bathroom for a drink, I looked in the mirror and all I saw was *this*." He wagged his sluggy arms around and pointed to his fat legs, greasy and slorping down in cascading layers of blubber.

"Then I felt famished and raided the fridge in the office, but it wasn't enough and I smashed open the vending machine down in the little game room the church has for the bored kids, and I ate every chocolate bar."

SICKNESS IN HELL

"Sounds like your day has been even stranger than ours. I was attacked by a bum and ended up eating him and then your priest attacked us both when I was at her house. She's my sister, by the way."

"Dawn, Dawn is my name." She stared sideways at Germaine. She always thought he might have mild autism because he didn't like to use names and because of his social awkwardness outside of deeply interpersonal settings."

"Like I said, I'm Adam the janitor, and I'm not paid enough for this crap."

"Half the town is dead" Germaine replied, "or probably more than that, we're here to burn the church, we thought maybe there were other freakazoids here that needed cremation."

"No need for those" the janitor said, pointing at the kerosine, "the church has its own gas generator. Let's just blow it sky high and forget about it. Or, we could always fortify it, it's a lot bigger and the walls a lot thicker than any house."

Germaine rapidly realized this was a good idea- if it had a generator they would have more reliable power, at least for a while, and the stone walls would be impenetrable to attack. They'd have to board up the lower windows in the offices though.

"I want to burn the church" his sister said, shifting

from leg to leg, bored out of her skull at the idea of residing in a temple.

"Let's burn something else, he has a point."

"Fine, but if I don't get to commit an act of arson today the day will be all for nothing."

In the next few minutes Germaine learned that Adam was a fan of cowboy movies and had been in the military. Both of these were good; he too liked a good Gunsmoke marathon and anyone who had learned the ways of combat was probably better as a friend than an enemy. He remarked that he'd never been in combat- just a technician in the navy- he knew how to defend himself though, and to illustrate this he started doing karate chops and kicking up his massive, bloated legs, stopping only when one sprang a leak and let loose a sizzling waft of gas and some sprinkling dots of tumor juice.

"That's horrific" Germaine remarked.

"How do you think I feel?" Adam cracked a smile.

It didn't take long to moderately defend the church. Adam had a taser and Dawn had her makeshift flamethrower and a ball bat. Germaine forsook the saber in favor of a hammer, which was potentially easier to wield fully in an enclosed area. The saber got stashed under the altar as they moved through the church; the one altar boy that was present was already dead, apparently predated upon by the priest they had slaughtered earlier.

SICKNESS IN HELL

Once some boards were nailed across the lower windows in the office section the work was basically done. They ripped up the seats in the main hall and stacked them off to the side to make room in the enormous arched area- then for good measure, hastily built a crossbar for the front door that could lock it more capably. While Germaine and Adam scavenged the building for various goods, Dawn went out and began indiscriminately burning down all the homes in the block, starting with the abandoned pile of wreckage (which went up like tinder, dry and ruined) and continuing around the church with each home, eventually forming a regular wall of flame that choked off visibility and burned down into cinder and left a significant no-man's land around the church, the graveyard, and the adjacent lawns which ran for about ten yards in front and back of the fenced area delineating the holy grounds and several acres on one side. On the other side was the side street so that counted also- after all, it was clear of visual obstructions.

Germaine still wanted to explore the processing plant even though it was still releasing puffs of steam or white smoke in the distance. The church was significantly closer to the plant than any of their homes was- Adam after all said he'd lived outside of Hillcrest and both Germaine and Dawn had lived on the other side of the town. They decided someone would have to stay behind to continue gathering goods, fortifying as needed, and most importantly to unlock the door when anyone returned. Adam wasn't too keen on wandering through streets that could be full of more maniacal priests, so he took up the saber and manned the bell tower with a pair of binoculars which the bishop (who must have been on vacation for neither his corpse nor his person was found to be on the grounds) had been storing in a box in the stairwell halfway up to the bell- an old brass affair smelted into existence before any of them were born. Adam got the idea that he would ring the bell if any significant attack took place so that Germaine and Lil' Sis could high-tail it back and help defend the location.

The fires which Dawn had set were already dying down when they left an hour later, but a few of them had managed to spread by ash and cinder through the air, igniting brush or outbuildings nearby. They passed a burning garage on the way through, and a dry, fallow field which had been partly burned also. Germaine derided his sister for lack of fire safety and she told him she'd throw him into the burning garage and eat his roasted corpse if he continued. He knew better than to perturb her further.

The edge of the plant where the road had once led to it was utterly, completely impassable- the explosion had cratered the earth and left a gaping hole some twenty feet deep topped with a high, slanted ring of jagged metal, loose concrete, and twisted tar which had been partly melted and apparently settled in place to melt down the sides of the whole thing. A piece of the plant on the other side, which had been crudely connected to the main factory by a walkway some twenty yards in length- leading from the factory floor and packing, that is, to the offices- was still intact, although the side of the building had sustained damage and the windows were gone, the side of the red brick now scarified with melted debris, coated in a thin layer of stinking ash, and blackened in places where fire had burned long and hard against its surface.

SICKNESS IN HELL

To enter this partly stable office complex they had to work their way around the crater, noting a prevalence of strange fungus growing on the swampy soil on the outer rim of the crater, where it almost extended into the swamps down below some fifteen feet through a sloped embankment which had once been green with grass, now ashen and withering, almost dead after only a few short hours. The vapor coming off of the crater was determined to be steam- the explosion had caused a major fire which had burned down to a smolder and was still vaporizing water which had pooled up in the lower levels of the building from the intake system. A huge shelf of mushrooms was down there too, as they peered over the sides of the ruined building, and it was growing so swiftly that they could actually hear the crunching noise of wet flesh on wet flesh as it strained its hyphae into the soil around the pooled water.

The office door had probably been locked but it had been almost blasted off its hinges by the pressure wave of the processing plant as it was hurled into oblivion, so they simply pulled it the rest of the way off, mindful that there might be the odd employee still inside sheltering in place- either unharmed or mutated.

The dim humming of a gas generator on the other side of the office explained why the lights were on, even if the fire alarm system was obviously not working, the absence of shrieking "shit's on fire, yo" noises belying the sad fate of whatever electrical system had been supplying them.

VI: OLD MRS. PILLWAFF

Germaine was cautious to work his way slowly through the offices. The building had been damaged enough on one side so that cracks and holes where debris had been fired right through the walls were letting in a small but decent amount of sunlight, that big ball of hydrogen in the sky waning towards its spot to set, aiming the light right through the damaged side. Because the building was filled with dust and ash which was dancing slowly around in the air, each beam shining through its respective hole or crack filtered through the particles hanging there like a solid rod of light.

Dawn was a bit less worried about stealth and much more excited than Germaine to explore the wreckage. Little bits of tree root, steel, brick, cooled cinder, and dirt, were scattered about the hallways and side rooms- indeed, the inner wall closest to the outer layer torn half apart by the explosion was itself substantially damaged, and some of the doors, which might otherwise have been locked tight, were ajar from the blast, their hinges damaged enough to simply rip them loose, the locking mechanisms no longer functioning as they might have the day before.

Part of the roof had apparently sunken in on itself and begun to sag in one corner of the area and water filtering through the debris above from ruined pipes had dripped down and begun to form strange formations resembling stalactites where the ash and cinder had coagulated into a crumbly substance not unlike the loose, porous volcanic soils of Cappadocia. On these little stalactites, it seemed, little stringers of musky-smelling fungus had begun to grow, and here and there, dotting them, and gathering in little patches on the floor where the water under the stalactites had pooled up in the dust colored carpets, were little colonies of mushrooms, off-white and shining in the sunbeams and dust, warm to the touch, literally thriving after only a few short hours in their chemically active abode.

Dawn figured it was a good idea to eat one and didn't regret the action; she reported that it tasted nutty and mild, and probably better than the mushrooms she often added to her pizza. Germaine thought the idea sounded strange, but everything was strange now, so he gobbled a little cap, disagreeing only on the nuttiness, but agreeing it was mild. Its flavor was perhaps akin to unseasoned white meat chicken.

Working their way past a group of stalactites into the back hallway which connected to the shipping area and to the underworks of the plant, they were interrupted by a massive crashing noise, which echoed through the fast-decaying building like the shot of a cannon. To them, it sounded like part of the building might just have given way, and they glanced at each other, in a non-verbal suggestion that perhaps the whole building would collapse and they might want to leave; but then a scratching noise followed a brief interlude of silence after the crashing noise, and Germaine was curious. Perhaps some sort of animal had wandered into the plant and just fell through a ruined spot in the floor, maybe he could eat the animal, roasting it alive after force-feeding it mushrooms. He almost salivated from the idea, not even realizing how monstrous a conceptualization it was that he had just envisioned.

The scratching continued along with an occasional thumping noise. Dawn busied herself as they walked through, mumbling to herself; she was displeased, for small, cystoid masses had clumped up on her ass, forcing her to reach inside her pants and pinch them off, squishing them into a stalactite- where they stuck to the side. As Germaine watched, the cysts were almost immediately consumed by the stalactites and absorbed completely in mere seconds, each one replaced by a freakishly fast-growing mushroom cap which sprouted up, opened, and released a blast of spores- or so the two of them took them to be, a mushroom-smelling faint dust which powdered the floor below.

Another crash resounded through the building and they took this to be a sign that something was alive several rooms away and, possibly, below them in the underworks. It didn't really matter though, Germaine's curiosity was giving way to one of those "bad feelings" and he wasn't about to stick around to tempt fate. He grabbed Dawn's arm and they turned around to go back the way they came, before an almighty crash sounded below them- and now the floor was crumbling away there, leaving a hole, which sunk down about half a foot around its sides, before a massive, bloated arm reached up through the opening, grabbing one of the steel beams sticking out sideways over the hole.

SICKNESS IN HELL

The hand on this bloated member fumbled around for a moment and then gripped the metal tightly, Germaine backing up, Dawn diving behind a table to the side, neither of them desiring to peer over the edge of the hole to see who owned the limb. With a white-knuckled grip, the arm appeared to try and pull whatever it was connected to out of the underworks, but failed as its fingers fell off- with a wet thumping sound, whoever was down there fell on their ass.

"Shit! Cockfucking shit!" A phlegmy, hoarse voice was shouting from below, this time releasing a shattering blast as it hurled something across the underworks, now stepping atop it and pulling itself half out of the hole. Germaine didn't recognize the woman now lurching there, her enormous flabby belly flopping around and pinching itself against the steel beam.

He took another step backwards, and the slug woman- for her jowls were so fatty that her facial features were mostly obscured in a layer of blubbery, greasy, pockmarked skin- garbled out something that mildly resembled speech, rearing her head back and coughing out a wave of phlegm which fired from her gullet like a sheet of water, dangling there as she wiped it loose with a wet, spongy sound, casting the lung fluid aside and ramming her right fist into the floor, trying to anchor herself and drag her bulk out of the underlevel.

"Fuck you bitch bastard whore!" She pounded the floor and flailed her other hand, dragging herself up and out by a half a foot or so, still apparently stuck there. "Help me out, before I grind you up and sell you!"

SICKNESS IN HELL

Dawn gave Germaine a knowing look- he nodded- it was the infamous plant owner herself, the perverted, eccentric, and begrudging owner of the Hillcrest factory- the last significant industrial baron of the entire county- Mrs. Pillwaff.

Only she seemed even more hideous than usual. The clown whore makeup and massive perfume scent she usually bore had been replaced by the smell of literal rotting meat- like a whole elephant, sectioned with a spiral saw, had laid out in the sun for a weekend and been roasted and served like a bubbling, syphilitic chunk of dead vagina, smelly and rancid. Instead of pancake makeup, she had the literal consistency of pancake drippings, uncooked and sedimentary, gooey like a glue or a vaguely unprocessed rubber product. Her flesh, in the light, as she slowly inched her way up out of the darkness, was a disgusting sight to behold- it looked like she'd gained a couple hundred pounds, and she seemed to be much taller too, even if her legs were like a pair of short, stubby tree stumps tapering at the knee and then expanding into gigantic fleshy cones at her ankles.

The situation worsened when she actually managed to heave her massive body up onto the floor, flailing there and apparently unable to rise from a lying position. Her pants had ripped apart as her weight grew, and what little was left to cover her ass was coated in a hideously filthy layer of rectal grime and fizzling entrail- a few little bits of intestine poking out the side of her partially exposed, soil-brown panties, burping forth a little fart here and there like a trumpet.

SICKNESS IN HELL

Germaine didn't really feel inclined to help this horrific gorgon up onto her feet, and she shrieked obscenities and managed to get into a crouch and very slowly rise, and now her true height was apparent- about seven feet all told, although her enormous fatty bulk made her look far larger. Her eyes looked like tiny black dots, hidden mostly behind several crepitating bulges of flesh both under and above them, these ridges of hardened tissue covered in blotchy patches, each one blistered as though she had been hit in the face by a blowtorch several times.

"You ingrate little shits, get out of my fucking plant!"

Germaine was mildly intimidated by her size, despite her apparent lack of mobility, and said nothing, gazing at this horror with awe, like he was watching an enormously obese lion gulp down and vomit a pile of gazelle guts. Dawn, though, was already on her feet, apparently escaping the notice of Pillwaff, who had been facing Germaine the whole time- she had her flamethrower still on her back but was hefting the baseball bat in its place, choosing, for the moment, a pragmatic defense approach.

"Fine, I'll throw you out myself!" The enormous woman lunged at Germaine, falling on her own belly and expelling a tidal wave of black chyme from her throat, managing only to injure herself. Germaine almost laughed at the spectacle, unaware of her distance because of the low light conditions- until Pillwaff grabbed his lower legs and gave a jerk, throwing him off balance and to the side, where he smashed into the wall halfway down, the ruined paneling giving way, leaving him there bent backwards over its edge as the fat interloper struggled against him, propping herself most of the way back up against the wall on one side, bringing her enormous, fatty arm back and smashing it down on his chest- Germaine almost laughed a second time, grinning because of the slug woman's weakness- but Pillwaff saw this and became even more enraged.

"Think it's funny turd-boy? I'll give you something to laugh about faggot!" She gave a half-hop and landed right on him, crushing him against the edge of the wall, right on his spine, pushing enough weight onto it to leave him unable to breathe, flailing his arms and dropping his hammer on the other side in a moment of panic.

Dawn, though, realizing there was not actual danger, didn't hesitate but for a second before bringing the bat upwards across Pillwaff's face- it smacked it like a fly swatter against a pile of lard, leaving a splotch of bluish bruise behind but failing to elicit so much as the momentary notice of slugula, who was busy slapping Germaine's face and pressing down to crush him into nonexistence. A few hits to the back and head with the bat at last managed to convince the slug woman that someone else was behind her, her half-ruined nervous system finally registering some sense of feeling from the injuries she was receiving. She turned and aimed her beady, fat-hidden eyes at Dawn and snatched at the bat the next time she swung, grabbing it and giving a few tugs. Lil' Sis realized that it was pointless to continue and her brother looked like he was going to asphyxiate, so she grabbed for the flamethrower and took a step back, flicking the igniter and releasing a short blast of fire into Pillwaff's face. Momentarily surprised, the fat woman didn't react until the heat caused her skin there to bubble and blister.

"Earrrrgh!" She threw her hands over her face and struggled up from the edge of the broken wall, off Germaine, and whirled around, waving her arms around. She proceeded to grab a broken chair and hurl it into a wall, beating her fists against it and bringing one stubby leg up to kick in Dawn's general direction. With glee, she released another blast of fire and this time managed to ignite Pillwaff's remaining clothes, the searing tendrils of fire lightly burning the outside of her flesh, releasing the scent of smoked human excrement. In a moment of sadistic realization, Dawn lunged forward a few steps and shoved the end of her flamethrower right up Pillwaff's ass as she released the valve, firing a burning vapor right inside her guts, blasting several intestinal lengths loose as the woman stopped completely, frozen on the spot.

Pillwaff stared, with eyes as wide open as could be achieved, in mid-pose, anchored to the spot, and then she began to shiver, and shake, and she closed her eyes and crouched slightly, balling her fists up, and let out a roar which was so phlegmy and so loud, and so prolonged, that Dawn feared her ears would bleed- as she roared, Pillwaff bent over a little more, and with an enormous splash, a gigantic wave of liquefied, burning crap came sloshing out under pressure from her anus, spewing across the floor along with a gigantic knot of apparently decaying gut

SICKNESS IN HELL

tissue- a ball of intestine, muscle, cyst, and hyphae which spilled out onto the carpet, emptying her bloated stomach altogether, as her flesh there, across her belly, went mostly slack, hanging down and drooping.

Dawn stood back in horror at the fact that the woman had just shit out her guts but failed to keel over in pain or, better yet, die altogether. Germaine had risen by this time, apparently not paralyzed or asphyxiated, and had retrieved his hammer from the other side of the gaping hole in the wall- he watched as well, astonished, as Pillwaff reached back with one stubby arm and squished it into her ass, frowning and making gurgling noises at them, mixing her hand around in that dirty hole, prolapsed and caked with grime, until she grabbed a length of her own intestine.

With a screech of pain, the slug woman attempted to bring the intestinal whip back and slam it into Dawn's face, missing by a foot- the wet organ slapped against the floor beside her and let out a little burst of malignant slime as she responded to this attempted attack by blasting Pillwaff again with fire- a quick burst to the face, which this time failed to harm or confuse her.

Germaine was rightfully mad- who was this fat woman to attack his sister and try to crush him with her bloated vagina-smelling body? He brought back the hammer from the side and slammed it nail-remover-first into her head, where it stuck, anchored in her skull. She turned and slammed him across the neck, sending him cascading across the hallway, her strength apparently growing now that her weight was so much reduced by shitting out her own internal organs.

"Enough." Dawn calmly clutched back the valve and began spraying not a burst but a torrent of flaming gas at Pillwaff, the searing stream of billowing hydrocarbons caking her entire body, as she let loose a phlegmy scream and turned around, bending over in agony and losing her footing, rolling halfway back to the hole she had crawled out from to begin with. With one last blast of fire, Dawn managed to get her to fall sideways in the hole and, with a squishing sound, Pillwaff fell on the exposed tip of a metal spoke sticking up out from the chunk of wall she had used to climb up in the first place, impaling her in the throat.

There, then, as Dawn looked over the side, was the half burned Pillwaff, still alive, but entrapped on a spike and still smoldering, smoke furling up from her charred flesh, her mouth opening and closing spasmodically as she laid there, her body bent at a sharp angle over a table with the wall against it, holding her neck and head up, and stretching them out from her slumping form.

Germaine peered over the edge too, having arisen from the floor, grinning at Dawn and smelling the cooked flesh scent rising from the dying slug woman. Her fat was now exposed to the smolder through several gaping wounds and her skin was beginning to thin and tear apart on the neck where it was being stretched. Dawn released one last quick blast of flame down onto her, searing some of her exposed fat so that it bubbled and dripped down, before they turned and made their way from the building.

SICKNESS IN HELL

"You know," Dawn remarked, as they exited and began working their way back around the dirt crater under the slowly setting sun, "we probably should have made absolutely sure she was dead."

"I don't want to be out when the sun goes down, it's obvious the neighborhood is full of crazy people."

He had a point, she saw- after the priest and now the slug woman, no telling what kind of other freaks were around.

"Why can some of them talk and some of them just seem crazy?"

"I'm not sure, whatever changed us must be different for different people. Maybe it's random."

They didn't talk at all while working their way around the rest of the mushroom-infected crater- the going was slow on the uneven and sometimes soft, sinky surface of the inundated dirt, and the inches of ash on top of them were surprisingly slippery to walk on- it required some degree of concentration. Around the time they had gotten back to the somewhat intact asphalt road, smoke began to furl out of the office building off to the side, and before they had made it to the edge of the property a bit of flame was rising up with a black, thin smoke that gave evidence to the efficacy of Dawn's arson capabilities. She was smirking as she watched.

"Well I guess I got to commit my arson of the day."

SICKNESS IN HELL

They didn't have long to tarry, and Germaine had to physically push her to get her to stop watching the fascinating demise of the last part of the processing plant that was at least partially intact. Thankfully, they met with no resistance on the walk back to the church, and when they got there, Adam had apparently abandoned his post at the belltower to begin plating the iron fence around the backside of the graveyard with wooden boards he was salvaging from the ruined property next to it, where Dawn's earlier arson had failed to fully destroy the debris.

"I figured it would make the yard more secure if things couldn't look up over it."

Germaine could find no argument with that- for a half hour or so they all began salvaging what usable wood they could find, and by the time it was no longer light enough out to safely work, half of the back end of the yard was enclosed by wooden boards which were not quite perfectly even but gave about six or seven feet of privacy screening. Dawn suggested they pull out the gravestones too, and use them to block the roads around the church property, and perhaps eventually dig in some spikes and pikes further out for a second layer of protection but both Adam and Germaine claimed that would be too much effort when they already had such a substantial area to fortify.

Lil' Sis ended up requisitioning the bishop's own bed, while Germaine and Adam took turns at the belltower that night, each one subsequently sleeping in the main room, literally on the altar of god itself.

VII. THE FAMILY

The subsequent morning began with a large amount of (slightly stale) coffee taken from the bishop's private food storage, with enough (perfectly fresh) donuts to kill an elephant with cholesterol. A philosophical discussion ensued- everyone there agreed that whatever had happened at the processing plant had caused their mutations, and it seemed likely, they believed, that the strange fungus Germaine and Dawn had encountered was the actual cause. Adam told them that his rudimentary understanding of water siphoning systems gave him a hunch that the intake had become clogged, leading to an explosion when some electrical system set off a spark or something, as trapped gas in the underlevel was ignited. He then posited that the fungus they had seen was a foreign element, maybe from the intake, but none of them knew where the water flow to the plant came from (none of them having worked there) so it seemed pointless to even discuss the topic.

The sun was barely peeking over the hills and beginning to saturate the countryside with an indirect glow slanted through trees and bushes when they all set to work again fortifying the iron railing around the yard- there was more wood than they thought, most of the planks and rods and odd sheets there in the dilapidated pile having been untouched by yesterday's fire. Germaine suggested that maybe they should leave the county and ask someone- maybe the police or something- what had happened and what to do.

SICKNESS IN HELL

His sister looked at him like he was nuts and he immediately reconsidered the idea- it did seem like a bad idea to approach a police officer or even a dog catcher when you're visibly mutated and fucked up.

"Yeah, my bad" he mumbled, busying himself with another plank.

The method of fortifying the iron railing was fairly easy but took twice as long as simply nailing sheets of wood to one another- the back side held the planks and sheets, the inside of the railing held small cross-bars of wood, bolted to the sheets on the other side from the interior so that the wood held fast to the railing. Dawn and Adam's sections looked perfect, but Germaine had always preferred theory to practice and his little compilation of planks was woefully uneven. As a joke he told them that the little gaps were for poking spears through at anyone too close to the wall.

"Why don't we get some more gas for the generator and I'll fiddle around with the radio system?"

Germaine glanced over to Adam, who was shuffling his puffy feet and gnawing on a chunk of cedar which he had requisitioned from the scrap wood, like it was the best-smelling thing he had ever encountered in all creation.

"What radio system?"

"The church had a cheap local broadcast, HAM radio, shortwave, probably has a range of a hundred miles, no more. Really low budget. There's a loop antennae in the top of the church and I've had to repair that stuff twice before."

"Why, so we can listen to music?"

"No, so we can try to communicate with someone not in the town, since everyone here seems to be dead or insane."

It seemed like a good idea. Germaine agreed to find propane while Lil' Sis and Mutated Janitor continued their struggle to build a heavily armed citadel and stave off the mutant horde. He knew right where to find it, too.

"I'll need my car."

He made his way through the dusty streets and back to his home where a feral dog had apparently died in the night in his lawn, its body reeking in the morning sun and swarming with flies, and a squirrel in the tree adjacent to the lawn wouldn't leave him alone as he went inside his home, driving him mad with its squirrel-speak. His keys were where he left them, and he piled the front seat of his sedan with some food and a few odds and ends- his shotgun, a first aid kit, and a flashlight and batteries- before clearing out some of the trash he'd had in the back seat and trunk, leaving it on the lawn beside the driveway. The squirrel continued to chitter at him, so he hurled a rock and managed to smash it in the head, the little vermin falling from the tree as limp as a dish rag. He grabbed it and shoved it in his mouth whole and still fresh, choking down

the morsel and gurgling with laughter. He might have
roasted and eaten the dog carcass but it looked just a little
bit too degraded and gassy for him to bother.

The only propane repository was helpfully called
"Jane's Propane" and was four blocks in the other direction.
It took him thirty seconds in the empty street to drive to it,
and soon the trunk was loaded with a pair of containers,
three more in the backseat, and a sixth next to him, almost
in his lap. Sure, it was an explosion hazard, but it didn't
phase him. It only took him a moment to crack apart the
little grating that protected the propane from thieves.

Someone was trapped inside the business, which
had apparently gone into lockdown mode the day before,
maybe because of the explosion, or maybe for some other
reason. He peered inside and a mildly deformed man was
pressed up against the window, drooling and riddled with
lumps and weeping sores, and he tapped on the glass,
causing the freak to turn towards him and begin gnashing
his sparse teeth, gobbling on his saliva-dripping jaw and
stumbling around. The glass was bulletproof, and the man's
pounding barely shook it. It took Germaine a moment to
decide whether to get in and blow him away with the
shotgun to put him out of his misery or to just drive off, and
he opted for the latter, too busy to bother.

On the short drive back Germaine saw that the fat,
mutated woman which had been stuck in her doorframe
across from Lil' Sis' house had achieved the impossible and
broken free. Standing naked in the middle of the road like a
hideous lump of lard, she waved and smiled as only a

kindly old granny could as he drove through, and began shuffling up the road after his car from a distance. Not knowing whether she was self aware anymore or was more like the priest he had killed or the bum he had eaten (or worse, self aware but nuts anyways like Pillwaff had been) he ignored her granny shuffles and maneuvered his car into the little opening in the rails behind the church- with a few attempts, for it was barely wider than his car- and delivered the needed propane.

"We might have a visitor, not sure if she's sane or not." He motioned up the road and Adam leaned over with a mildly concerned expression.

"Well, she doesn't look very mobile, just crush her skull if she goes mad or something, maybe."

Dawn didn't seem to like the plan and wanted to grab her flamethrower and mow granny down right in the road and had to be talked down from the idea. "We can't just destroy everything in town, if she's still sane that's another person for our little village here." She saw the reason in Germaine's words and relented, but appeared to hold her hammer a little tighter anyways.

Granny, still naked and dripping ooze from her ass with every step, managed, with some degree of difficulty, to shamble across the grass and to the fence, and began barking out an incoherent mass of squeaking and chugging noises and ended up communicating with gestures when she couldn't be understood.

SICKNESS IN HELL

They had no idea what was wrong with her- she seemed sane and wasn't attacking anyone, but couldn't speak.

"What's your name?"

More incoherence spilled out like the mumbling speech of an autistic lemur, but Germaine could see something Dawn and Adam had missed. Reaching forwards with one arm, he grabbed the old woman around the neck and slammed his other hand into her face, wriggling it around for a moment. Dawn looked on, believing that Germaine was trying to smother her or rip her skull out from her head, and cracked a malicious half smile.

After a moment Germaine withdrew his hand and held, there in his palm, what looked like a rock. The old woman keeled forward and gasped, and continued to gasp there for a good thirty seconds as he stood there agape at the spectacle.

"Can you speak?"

"Oh yes sweet boy, I feel much better now."

In between heady gasps the old woman explained the problem. After mutating she had been stuck in the door frame and had become so hungry she attempted to eat a rock, but had gotten it stuck in her throat.

"I thought I'd die but I just kept on living, as soon as I got light headed I felt a mighty pain in my back and then

73

this happened." She turned around and above her drippy asshole were two long sets of what appeared to be amphibious lung slits- apparently she had mutated to get oxygen when her normal method of breathing had become useless.

"I'm still mighty hungry by the way, you can call me Gran, all my seven grandkids did."

Gran proceeded to eat several cans of baked beans and chortled as she farted out the gas she obtained. Germaine considered telling her to fuck off but then she waddled down the road yammering something about canned goods and baked items. His ears perked up at the mere mention of baked goods; he had a soft spot for the finer cakes, pies, and muffins of the world. From their spot there at the church they couldn't see her but they could hear a distant banging- probably the old woman entering her home unable to do so through the door. Maybe she had a garage she could enter.

A little puddle of poo was left behind when she left, and little drops of poo dotted the road behind her in her voluminous wake. The scent was slightly sweet, which Adam remarked was odd; maybe she was diabetic. The scent was attracting some odd visitors, though.

There on the other side of the little grass area was a dog; not a friendly looking one either. It loped around with its muzzle to the ground, intermittently watching Dawn off to one side, Germaine and Adam watching the dog- it wasn't mutated, or so it seemed, just hungry and generally displeased at the state of the world. With a little grumbling it trodded across the road and Adam swung a piece of sheet wood in the way of the one gate they were making, so that it would be no easy task for it to enter their little grave-courtyard. With a howl, the dog lunged up onto the wood and almost got over it, flipping off its paws back a few feet only to try again- it wasn't an enormous shoulder-high bone shredding breed like an Irish Wolfhound or a muscle bound skull cracker like a Pit Bull, but it was large enough so that Germaine had to reach an arm around to steady the wood.

Another predator though seemed to be attracted. What crawled out of the little wooded area off to the side of the scrap heap was far larger and more monstrous- it seems cats were able to be mutated for sure, because what stood there observing, with astonishing passivity, the scene before it, was at least shoulder height and maybe larger. Maybe it had consumed its own owners, maybe it had been feral to begin with- whatever the case, the hulking shape that slowly pranced with great agility out of the treeline was terrifying to Germaine (who had no great love of cats) and merely interesting to Dawn and Adam, who were just as distracted as the dog trying to enter the courtyard, which turned around and lowered its head with small, grizzly eyes, surveying this new opponent.

The giant cat was at least seven feet from head to tail, and as scrawny and bony as physically possible- its ribs were so drawn against its skin that they protracted the latter, heaving with each breath, its face almost entirely defleshed save for a few lines of knotted muscle down each side of the jaw and below the ears, connecting the enormous musculature under and beside the jawline to the neck with grotesque efficiency. There was little skin here, they observed, as it tip-toed towards the dog, making no sound at all- worse, its feet had mutated from oh-so-cute little cat paws into knotted stubs covered in apparently vestigial connective tissues, each knot ending in a barbed claw the side of a meathook. Around said claws were tufts of extremely long hair like that on a well kept Clydesdale.

The dog lunged and was almost immediately sorry it did- its natural desire to chase things that smell like cats produced the opposite of the intended outcome and the gigantic feline took one swipe and skewered the oncoming canine in the face, dragging it to the side along the tar, pulling it up off the ground in both front paws, and slamming it down so hard that it was sent rolling several feet into the scrubby stalk of a rose bush. With the strength of a lion, the monstrous beast pounced straight down on the dog, smashing it with all four paws and digging in, literally engulfing the dog's entire head with its mouth, giving a little twist and bearing down, hunched over the corpse and seemingly sucking out its blood. After a minute or two the visibly withered corpse was left there to rot, empty like a bag of flesh with the organs and fluids drained away, and it laid down beside its prey as though proud of itself.

The little wooden wall, even if fully completed, wouldn't have kept the cat out, and Germaine and Adam already had their respective hammers ready, not that they expected such tools to be much use against something able to puncture their chest cavities with one swipe and rend them open.

SICKNESS IN HELL

Dawn had a different idea and was fascinated by the animal, cooing at it like it was nothing more than a housecat. Germaine warned her off in a low voice, convinced she'd do something stupid, and his warning went unheeded- stupid was just what she did, slowly bending down and doing the typical "aw you precious smooshy kitty cat" act and beckoning like she wanted to give it a belly rub.

Big kitty seemed interested more in eating dog corpse than being "smooshied", and started to bite its paws like a feisty cat will always do, only with this feline the sound made was like two bones clanking together as its huge fangs and its razor sharp cat claws struggled together. With a twitch of its tail, it suddenly hunkered down and whipped its tail back and forth and took a leap over the wall, right in front of Dawn. Germaine lifted his hammer, ready to attack, but the cat rolled over in front of her and purred so loud the ground almost vibrated.

"Awwwwww cats never change" she stroked its hairless face and then its stomach, grabbing one of its paws and doing twiddly things with its foot hairs. One look at the footpads showed them the extent of mutation; normally kitty cat has soft little pink footsies, this kitty cat had gigantic crenelated grooves on its feet pulsing with vascularity, as though its body had difficulty feeding enough nutrients to these important combat features.

Adam chuckled and went back to work, feeling the threat was over, but Germaine was so surprised at what he was seeing that he just stood there with a partially slack jaw and the hammer, forgotten, loosely clinging to his partially opened hand. He'd seen some weird shit in the last couple of days but this took the cake.

The cat wandered over and rubbed against Germaine's leg, almost knocking him over, and licked his hand with a tongue large enough to lap up a cup of milk in one go. He reached out and petted its neck a little and it curled its back upwards, happily, snuzzling him all the way from waist to face and this time managing to knock him on his ass. The happy cat then went over to some catnip plants growing among the gravestones and busied itself with getting high- something Germaine would probably be doing right now if the world weren't like one big hallucination already.

"Don't worry, I have cat-power" she said, laughing like a maniac and handing Adam some more framing for the eventual gate.

"I'm more worried that you *do* have cat powers."

"Don't worry ooty booty brother" she wagged a finger at him and took on a patronizing tone "we'll find you doggy woggy to pet, you like that? Baby little puppers?"

He ignored her and turned his back, partially embarrassed at his own fear, partly chuckling- maybe he *would* go find a pet of his own, hell maybe there was a mutant cow he could ride around or a giant amphibian he could fuck or something.

SICKNESS IN HELL

Gran came waddling back down the road around the time the gate was complete- it didn't take long, it just needed to be reinforced with a second layer of wood, now they could mount it, probably on the railing itself since the black iron was held up every six feet or so by sturdier, larger posts in between lengths of normal fencing.

She was toting a literal wagon full of goods- There was a cake, a few dozen cupcakes, a couple of pies, and what looked like fresh bread of at least two types- some sort of dark brown pumpernickel rye and another resembling wheat but with frosting on it, which turned out to be a fruitcake of some sort.

"I was planning a big day with the family, but I don't think it's going to pan out, and now I'm going to need help with all this stuff." She lifted out a cupcake and scarfed it down with horrific speed, smashing the little treat into her maw and cackling like she was temporarily insane. The smell wafting up from the wagon was more than a little enticing, and Adam was already tying into the fruitcake, remarking on it being a lot more moist than the ones you get in a store.

Dawn grabbed a whole pie and, seeing it was blackberry, fairly fawned with delight. He tried to grab a slice but she spirited it away into the building and wouldn't share, so he had to make do with curling up next to a gravestone near the cat and piling cupcakes down his gullet. "I still have two more wagon loads to bring." Gran said, grinning ear to ear as Germaine looked on.

SICKNESS IN HELL

VIII. SLOW PROGRESS

In the subsequent days slow progress was made in improving the situation. Germaine departed the others briefly in order to scout around outside of Hillcrest and see if he could ascertain what was going on, to see if, perhaps, the disaster which had screwed them all up was merely a local thing or, as he worried, if some sort of weird epidemic was busy laying waste to the world. The radio in his car wasn't receiving any signals from local stations or even regional ones, and the only things buzzing through were some international shortwave broadcasts on the HAM radio Adam had rigged up- nobody on any of these programs mentioned what had happened except for some ranting preacher who was shouting about the end times and how the government was hiding things from them- the broadcast had referenced "A disaster they won't talk about" and Dawn had put two and two together and suggested maybe Germaine was right to want to go seek out life outside of the town but "be careful and don't approach anyone, just observe."

Gran and Dawn scouted the surrounding neighborhood for food and supplies and found that more or less everyone in Hillcrest was dead in their homes- whatever had been released the death toll was freakishly high. Other than a mutated rat the size of a basketball and just as fat and bloated they saw no significant signs of life beyond plant or insect in the two blocks surrounding the churchyard.

SICKNESS IN HELL

Adam decided to set up a broadcast of his own, to seek out survivors which may be tuned into a radio broadcast. The station he had rigged up only had enough power to reach the edge of the county and perhaps a few miles beyond- for on three sides the area, sloping down from Hillcrest itself, ran off in every direction for twenty miles or so of rolling plains and foothill only to reach back up like the asshole of the devil, creating a wall of hills around the county which was higher than their own hill itself. On the fourth side, the broadcast would maybe go a bit further, since a river valley there extending roughly Northeast and Southwest ran diagonally for several miles before adjoining the hills around the county at the southern end, bending off into the hinterlands, and running in the opposite direction North for about ten miles before connecting to several smaller rivers and a lake.

It was that valley that Germaine figured he'd explore- if whatever had happened was contained at all it would have spilled out into that valley and he figured that might be protective- after all if everyone there was mostly dead, and the area was infected with some sort of deadly fungus that didn't affect him or the others, hopefully no foreigners would be there with their guns at the ready to mow him down on sight.

They all agreed that it was almost certain that the government knew by now generally what was happening, especially if the explosion had scattered infection downwind for some distance- what wasn't clear is whether this infectious fungus passed from person to person. Adam had a theory here.

SICKNESS IN HELL

"It obviously infects humans and cats and probably other mammals." He said. "Even if it doesn't transmit like a virus, if it kills someone and someone else comes into contact with the body, I believe it would infect them. The explosion probably hurled the infection at least to the end of the county line and by now it's probably well beyond that. Honestly I think it will be the next black death."

Germaine almost hoped that was the case- at the very least they could count on a few mutated survivors being present, at least a few of which were hopefully not insane and not ax murderers or something like that. Then again, Dawn was an arsonist in training so it's not like beggars can be choosers of their company.

"I'll try to be back within two days" Germaine told them all, "I'll leave my car at the edge of the town, I don't want to make a bunch of noise and find that the county is surrounded by the army or something with orders to firebomb anything trying to leave."

With one last hug Dawn ushered him off. He had a backpack and some food and a handgun he had requisitioned along with the saber, figuring if he ran out of bullets it was better than nothing if he was in a tight spot. His car had thankfully been fully fueled up the day before the explosion hit so he had more than enough gas to drive several hundred miles if need be.

As he pulled off and drove away, Adam climbed back into the loft and immediately began broadcasting, figuring he'd do so for two hour stretches a couple times a day. Dawn asked why he didn't just record a message and run some sort of computer program next to the microphone and leave it on constantly. He thought it sounded like a good idea.

"We're going to need more propane and we're going to need to consider getting some solar panels or something up here when the gas runs out."

Dawn remembered how she'd read about a solar project just south of the plant which had been partially installed a month before. "You're the one that knows about engineering and stuff, do you want me to come with you? Might need a pickup to grab a couple panels."

"I'll go alone, I have a shotgun so it should be all good."

He departed as well, smashing the window of a blue pickup truck across from the church still in the driveway of someone's home. He smashed the door down with a hammer and managed to find their keys, still clutched in the hand of a now grizzly, moldy corpse, blotchy and blue and covered in dried blood which had trickled from its mouth not two days prior. The pickup had just enough room for his puffy legs, but he had to squeeze them in anyways and got a roll of fatty tissue caught in the door, yanking it free with a sickening snap. The wound healed immediately but almost instantly began giving him hunger pains- he smashed a cupcake into his mouth. "That will have to do for now" he chuckled, speeding off to the south side of the old industrial sector.

SICKNESS IN HELL

Upon Adam's departure, which was, between smashing a window and speeding off in his vehicle, quite noisy, a pair of eyes perked up in a home not far from the church- behind the inner row of homes, next to a garage which had been partially immolated. These eyes watched Gran and swiveled around to gaze at two other sets of eyes there, all of them furrowing half closed as these three beings lurched out of the darkness of their ruined bedroom and through the home, out onto the street.

With Germaine and Adam both gone the area was vulnerable; true, a giant cat was helping to guard things there, but four people and a giant cat beats two people and a giant cat any day. The beings crawling forth from the building there were almost otherworldy, especially the one which seemed to be in charge. Dawn saw them first, as they crossed through the lawns there and headed towards the street separating "their" land from that outside and unguarded.

The first being, a grizzly head taller than the others, was like a giant grub of sorts- or rather an old man with a long, grotesque beard soaked in his own blood, who had mutated so severely that his back legs had been completely surrounded by his gut, which now dragged on the ground like the abdomen of a fleshy insect. With each shuffling movement, on his enormous arms, which were leathery and coated completely in hair, he flopped his gigantic body up and down, undulating across the lawn and onto the road, which was apparently displeasing to him- he roared as he made contact with it, rolling onto his side and dislodging a sharp rock from his skin.

SICKNESS IN HELL

One of the other beings was tall and thin, almost like a lich or something akin to it- an unsteady-looking and warped being with an elongated face and holding a crowbar in one knobby hand. The third being was not that grotesque, just a woman whose breasts had apparently sunk down to her ankles and become an extra set of arms, replete with hands of their own, although they were malformed and had too few fingers, so that they resembled the talons of a vulture. Her face was badly burned and her lips were missing- this didn't prevent her from shrieking at Dawn and Gran, alerting also their new pet to the presence of interlopers.

The fat one had a rifle and almost immediately opened fire, forcing Dawn to dive behind the wooden wall and Gran to crouch down, smiling and grabbing a cupcake as though it was a weapon, ready, Dawn determined, to perhaps attempt to choke the enemy. Their cat was unafraid of any being but was terrified of the noise the rifle made and scrambled off so fast that it had difficulty gaining enough traction on the loose grave dirt to run in any given direction. With a few whirls of its tail for balance the beast made way like a cheetah across the yard and behind the church, disappearing entirely.

Abandoned by perhaps their most formidable defense mechanism, Dawn tossed her flamethrower to Gran and huddled there with her hammer, prepared to hook it in the face of anything approaching the wall. Through a few little odd slits in the wood where it was uneven she observed the advancing squad of mutants.

SICKNESS IN HELL

"Food time!" The fat man bellowed, flopping and undulating his hideous obesity with greater intensity, farting with each movement of his belly corpulence.

"Yes, food!" Gran countered, tossing a cupcake over the side of the wall to the oncoming force. Dawn looked sideways at her like she was suffering from a bout of dementia and wasn't aware of the danger, but as she turned back to watch the approaching horde, she got to see the fat man bend down with great excitement and what looked to be slight confusion, picking up the cupcake with his fat fingers with extreme dexterity, moving it back and forth and holding it up to the sun like it was a delicate treasure, before scarfing it down. A vague and temporary look of fear crossed his face for a moment as he tasted it, mashing it around his mouth as though checking it for poison. He stopped moving entirely and continued to look confused, like someone had just posed a riddle so strange it had cracked his mentality altogether.

"Gran?"

"Peter?"

The old woman stood up from her spot with almost a little too much speed and reeled forward, having to catch herself on the side of the treat wagon. "I knew it was you you silly man!"

"Gran, I thought you were dead, you weren't in your home!"

SICKNESS IN HELL

Dawn stood up slowly still holding the hammer. "Who the hell is this?" She alternated between glancing at the old woman with confusion and in the other direction with some degree of alarm. It wasn't clear what relationship existed between these two but she'd just been shot at and wasn't going to take the mere word of anyone unwilling to offer an explanation of why she shouldn't feel a bit unnerved.

"Ohhhh this is my stepson Peter, dear, nothing to worry about."

Peter looked less like a human being and more like a gigantic maggot and Dawn was not entirely convinced that letting her guard down was a good idea.

"Sorry about that miss" he croaked, through fatty, compressive lungs, "I didn't know y'all were friendly, but I can tell one of Gran's cupcakes any day. I didn't even see her and didn't want to take chances on being eaten. We had to kill one crazy woman this morning who tried to gnaw on us, tried to come through a window."

Feeling only slightly relieved, Dawn was willing at least to lower her hammer, after all the man could have shot her the moment she rose if he had wanted to.

"I'm Dawn, so, who are these others?" She pointed to the slender fellow with the deer-like muzzle and the burn victim.

"Oh, my son and daughter ma'am, we were sleeping

in that house over there last night but something burned it down and we had to escape back through the woods. We didn't want to go into the street and get attacked or something. Also, do you know what's going on? Why is everyone dead? Why are we like this?" He pointed to his belly and his son's apparent disfigurement with the self awareness marking a sentient being.

Dawn didn't have the heart to tell him that in all likelihood, it was one of the fires she had started that scarified and charred his daughter's face. "We're not sure what's happened beyond that the processing plant exploded and within hours everyone was either dead or fucked up. My brother and I explored the plant and it's full of weird fungus of some sort, we think it infected people. He's exploring the edge of the county, and there's another man here who is getting some solar cells for a radio broadcast too."

Peter thought about the whole situation for a moment and then began sobbing miserably. With his obesity and deformity it caused his whole body to shake and ripple with wavering currents of liquid-under-membrane hideousness. Dawn almost immediately felt very sorry for this poor, malformed wretch, who she had formerly feared was a lunatic.

"M-my wife gone." Was all he managed to sputter in his incoherent grief. With another wracking wave of tears he also vomited all over the ground, which was almost as disgusting as watching the expressionless, fire-scorched face of his daughter staring at the vomit and sticking her tongue out repeatedly in a crude manner. The burn victim patted her father on the shoulder and slender son tried and failed to bend down far enough to hug him.

Gran helpfully offered them food which was still plentiful- she reminded them all that more was still at her house and that there was probably an unlimited supply able to be scavenged elsewhere, not to mention all the local farms which had corn and other things to spare. This perked Peter up, and soon he was lounging uselessly next to the food while his children aided Dawn in shoring up the wall. While apparently a mute due to deformity, his son turned out to be remarkably good at strategic planning and used some paper and a pen to relate his ideas to them all- starting with a second wall around the church with a small ditch on the outside and a couple of gates which they could make from garage doors. It would be difficult, but it would give them a much larger area to operate safely in. She was still miffed that their cat was gone, at least briefly, until the beast reappeared and, seeing the danger had passed, went and laid down next to Dawn with a sullen look, neither happy nor alarmed at these newcomers' presence.

Adam meanwhile was having a great time. His skin was too leathery for mosquitoes to bite him, and as he sloshed through the slightly inundated soil around the cheap solar field south of the processing plant, he chuckled frequently because the biting insects of the world had always been attracted to him. Swatting the little bastards, he ended up eating them as they were crushed against his almost carapace-like flesh.

SICKNESS IN HELL

It took a good long time to take the panels down such that they were inert when he disconnected and loaded them. He got the idea that if a black tarpulin was placed over them first, that at least he wouldn't be instantly ass blasted if he did something wrong or accidentally made contact with the wrong component and was electrocuted. His theory turned out to be a good one; at two separate points he did indeed get shocked, but the current was too weak to do anything substantial.

His choice of vehicles was nothing short of miraculous as well; the pickup had six of the tarps in the back and the bed of the pickup was almost exactly the same length as the cells themselves; once loaded all he had to do was wedge some cardboard in the back and they wouldn't move. With the tarps protecting them and some rope to keep them from jostling too much, it took a few hours but the entire thing was perfectly arranged; that would give just enough juice to broadcast during the day, and if he could set up a battery system they could broadcast at night-moreover there were still dozens of panels left that could be taken at any time and used for something else- probably lamps and maybe some space heaters for the winter time.

The solar field was harvested and Adam was getting hungry again, taking a hidden slab of apple pie from his pocket, smooshed together and covered in pocket dust and hair, and rammed it in his gullet at the same time that he got back in the pickup. He immediately felt far better, and with his load intact decided to head back to the church- it would take a good week just to figure out how to mount the panels but he had all the time in the world.

SICKNESS IN HELL

Germaine's progress was much more slow. The recent rains had flooded a small stream over the dirt road he had chosen to walk on in lieu of the paved main thoroughfare, thinking if he was in a completely rural setting surrounded by trees that he could approach the edge of the county without significant risk of being seen. After a half an hour of walking across this idyllic landscape he realized that his path was impeded. It took fifteen minutes for him to walk upstream to a spot wide enough and shallow enough to cross and then his shoes and his pants up to the knee were soaked completely, making continued walking a bit less entertaining and a bit uncomfortable. He ended up taking his shoes off altogether and hurling them into the woods in a mild fit of rage, choosing to go barefoot- after all his feet were somewhat larger and harder than they used to be, almost like they were their own pair of shoes.

At the edge of the woods where the bare dirt road met the slope of the valley, some two hours later, he got onto his belly and began crawling to the treeline, figuring if ever there was a spot that would be likely to be guarded, it was this one. He managed to squirm along the side of the road through the brush until he was perched behind a log and was able to raise his head just a little to take a gander around and see what he could see in the hills and sloping fields beyond.

He didn't observe any immediate danger but his caution kicked in and he figured it would be best to stay put for a good twenty minutes or so and just observe the hillsides and see if, perhaps, any substantial movement could be seen thereupon. A few cupcakes later he hadn't seen anything still and became slightly impatient.

He rose up partially and hunched over to another tree, still gazing and seeing nothing of note, and figured maybe there was nobody guarding anything at all- maybe the world had basically ended and the infection had already decimated everything immediately beyond the county as well. Seeing this lack of danger he ventured beyond the trunk by a few feet, standing upright and breathing a sigh of relief.

A sudden pain struck out from his left shoulder and then he heard the crack of a bullet fired from some distant location. Alarmed and reeling he turned and swung around back behind the tree. His shoulder was bleeding but not badly, and another crack followed, a bullet whizzing by and smacking the next trunk over, taking a bite out of it. It seemed he was being observed after all.

Suddenly, a din filled his ears and for a moment everything shook and blurred to white. When his vision had corrected, his ears were ringing loudly and he had been upended, stunned, and was on the ground not ten feet from a smoking crater with dust furling up about it. In the distance, upon a hill not a mile ahead of him halfway across the valley, was a little puff of gray smoke where a field cannon had let loose a shot in his direction. Another puff of smoke came from a spot beside it and he could see the second cannon there, and then with a massive banging noise, he blacked out.

IX: A DEAL WITH THE DEVIL

After a day of waiting for Germaine the others had
become a bit nervous- true, it was quite a walk and Dawn
fully expected that he'd be gone more than a day if it turned
out that nothing short of armageddon was upon them and
the entire region was depopulated completely, but
something in the back of her mind was gnawing away at
her and told her that something, whatever it was, was
amiss. She decided that she would go out after him, at least
to the same general area he'd said he intended to explore.
Adam remarked that he would go with her but supplying
power to their little citadel was quite a task- he was still
trying to figure out how to get the solar cells to the roof,
and had rigged them up on the little flat area on top of the
offices, where they were stable and up off the ground but
received little other than shadow from the side of the
church in the morning hours, which was only temporarily a
decent arrangement. The others were all working feverishly
on the plan concocted by Peter's lanky son, whose name
turned out to be Alex; it was going well too, one side of the
new embankment had been dug out and once the digging
was done the wall would go up, at least if they had the
materials to do so.

She wondered if she should take her pet cat- after
all there was probably no better defense than a being just
shy of a sabertooth tiger for personal protection, but if their
little citadel was raided the others would probably need the
help, and she didn't feel like coming back to a smoldering
crater where the church had once been, only to have to

hunker down in an unpowered suburban home with no food or lights on. She opted for requisitioning the rifle instead, figuring it would be just as good, and took her hammer too for good measure. It was barely morning when she departed, leaving the others to their various work.

Germaine awoke miles away to complete and abject darkness. He laid there in the dark realizing something was wrong and decided to sense what was around him in the seemingly silent void; it felt like he was laying on slightly moist, warm stone, or maybe brick. He could hear a trickle like water percolating down a wall, and in the distance something echoing although he couldn't quite put his finger on it. His body may have mutated to do many things but his vision was no more adept than it ever was before, and he arose from wherever he was laying before, feeling around with his feet and hands and figuring he was in a cave or a tunnel of some kind, very slowly creeping off the surface he was on and feeling a floor beneath him, more or less level in shape, putting his weight down and feeling around some more.

It seemed he was in a very small alcove or something like unto an alcove- with his hands he felt the wall, slowly moving about until he felt what seemed to be an opening no higher than five feet or so which passed into a tunnel. Taking this route, bent over double, he held one hand to the side to keep feeling the wall, the other above and before him to prevent himself from smashing his head on the low hanging ceiling. He crept through this tunnel, the echoing in the distance bouncing off the walls and disorienting him somewhat.

SICKNESS IN HELL

After several minutes the echoing beyond him became notably louder, and continued to slowly grow in its din until it was a regular cacophony- he could hear voices in this echoing, ringing mess of sound, but none of them were distinguished from any other. The tunnel began to narrow slightly but he could see a dim light perhaps twenty yards beyond and off, it seemed, to one side or the other. As he got closer the sound magnified even more until he really wanted to use one of his hands to cover his ears- then he emerged around this corner and ten feet beyond was a large opening, and what he saw beyond this made him stand there in shock.

There, before him, so it seemed, was literal Hell itself. There was a little stony path in front of him which ran infinitely to either side, along an enormous canyon of stone, down below, at least a hundred feet below him- and this canyon was filled with running humans and hovering demons alike, twisted and grotesque, some monstrous in shape and form, belching hideously and attacking anything that moved. Enormous rocky stalactites dripping from the high, almost vaulted ceiling of stone above, some two hundred feet, met stalagmites growing upwards in the opposite direction, and there were, it appeared to him, quite a few bridges of rock spanning the canyon, leading off to paths on both sides of the region, in seemingly random directions. Holes in the wall along these paths, connected by these bridges, were little more than voids of blackness clinging in between the crags of stone there, ridged and weathered with age.

The air here, unlike in that of the tunnel he had

emerged from, was hot and moist, like the mist of a swamp draining upwards into a poisoned atmosphere, releasing a vague foulness into his nostrils that didn't make him gag but did make itself noticed. He watched the frantic people below and the guffawing demons for a short while; some were almost diminutive, like demonic little midgets with leathery wings flapping about, shrieking or laughing, hurling rocks at one another, the people below, or the walls in what seemed to be a confused frustration.

There were other creatures too- there was some sort of gigantic spider on the wall surrounded by a web, perched there with its legs outstretched over one of the bridges, partly hidden by a pair of stalactites one on either side of it- this enormous spider waited there as Germaine watched, until a demon came running across the span, and it reached out like the crack of a whip and swung the being around and hurled it up into the web, where the screaming devil stuck, wriggling and trying to escape. As the spider bent in to envenomate or devour it, the demon apparently stuck it in the eye with a sword or some other sharp object, because the venomous arachnid reeled back and flailed one side of its legs down into the open air over the span, actually falling, suspended by its own silk, which was like a literal rope of sticky residue. The confused animal tottered off to the side and back up across the stalactite onto its web and shook the demon loose, thinking better about trying to eat it.

A roar from Germaine's side told him someone was coming, and up across the ledge came a whole squad of demons, each in black armor, carrying hideously deformed weapons, not forty feet down and away from him. He slunk back into the hole, into the shadowy void as they approached, but the demon in front, who was perhaps a couple of inches taller than the others, and almost as tall as Germaine, reached back into the hole and grabbed his hand, yanking the frightened mutant out into the light again, turning him around and choking him against the wall. His face was dripping with demon sweat and covered in dusty ridges and wrinkles like that of an extremely geriatric coal miner, and he stopped, emotionless, for a moment, glaring at Germaine, before cracking a surprisingly sweet smile.

"Welcome to Hell, you have been expected. We are all very excited for your arrival, mister Woodsworth."

Germaine almost wanted to ask why he was in Hell, then remembered briefly that he had cannibalized a hobo not too many days ago, figuring he was about to be thrown in a pit of magma or fed to the spider. Then what the demon had said sunk in; he was expected? The demon was excited?

"Excited?"

"Yes." The demon released him, seeing Germaine hadn't tried to run or maybe pole-ax him in the head. "Our master has been watching you, the time draws near."

"What time?"

The demon's grin turned into an elated howling laugh so loud that the wrinkled, grisly being choked on his own spittle and gagged, reeling backwards and steadying himself by grabbing the crotch of the demon next to him so he wouldn't teeter and fall over the side of the ledge, which after all lacked a railing and was precarious at best.

"Hahaha! Oh man." The demon was so amused that he ignored the question and slapped Germaine's back, leading him down the path and intermittently chuckling, then burst out laughing yet again as the others with him bore shit eating grins and were wracked with laughter that they suppressed, literally biting their tongues- literally- for several fleshy little red sections of tongueflesh dotted the path behind them, laying there and still wriggling on the stone floor.

"Oh man, wait until we get there" the demon chuckled uncontrollably again, "this is going to be better than Pol Pot."

Germaine was confused beyond his ability to continue questioning the unhelpfully amused demon, and the one behind him was prodding him in the ass with a dagger and laughing about it, so he saw no point in bothering any conversation. This made the subsequent trip somewhat more boring than it could have been, because they ended up walking for two hours.

After the canyon was left behind the host passed through a sort of giant iron gate which stood near the top of the high ceiling, connecting to the stone paths on either side of the canyon walls, which expanded and widened until they were a good ten yards from edge to wall, sloping gently up to the black gate, which stood there decorated with an unusually colorful assortment of gemstones which glinted and shone from the light of torches placed around it. The dim reddish glow of the canyon behind them, Germaine observed, seemed to be a sort of phosphorescence and not from a typical light source at all, for the torches were the only obvious lighting in the entire expanse.

Beyond the gate the path took them through an extremely wide tunnel, which seemed to be lined with enormous rib bones of some sort or another, which terminated at the peak of the ceiling in a series of joints very much like a backbone- and he could hear a rumbling in the distance, trying as they walked to get a good look at what was off to each side, where the rib-tunnel was lined with openings about the size of normal doors, each one containing, beyond it, he saw, rooms where groups of demons were sitting and eating, or chatting with each other.

An enormous slug, like those in any garden or swamp, churned by them as they continued, its slimy eyes rotating freely, leaving a half inch slick of slug juice as it passed. One of the demons stepped half in the slick and fell on his face, eliciting more laughs.

"You retarded, clumsy oaf." The head demon was less amused than the others and grabbed the wretch from the floor, where even his face had landed in the slug glue, and yanked him up with one muscly arm, throwing him to the other side. "Watch where you walk."

SICKNESS IN HELL

They left the main tunnel behind and proceeded left down through a gate larger than the doors which had lined the hall behind them, onto a winding staircase which wound around and around like a spiral, down at least five hundred steps, or so Germaine counted- at the bottom was a fairly small round room and on one side of the rounded wall, another opening, which led into an antechamber no bigger than the average bedroom, on one side of which was a pair of doors which seemed to be made from solid silver.

"Go in, good sir, the master awaits."

Germaine had a pretty good idea that he was about to meet Satan or something like that, and shuddered a little bit, figuring maybe this was some sort of Hellish hazing ritual and he was about to get sentenced to ten thousand years of hard labor shoveling giant spider shit or cracking rocks with a pickax to build a chamber full of lava that he would then be tossed into. He cracked the doors apart and walked through, and wasn't expecting what he saw there.

This room was quite unlike what had come before- it was a strange place, with a flat, rectangular ceiling, and enormous mahogany pillars running up each wall, between which an extremely annoying hot pink paint was plastered on perfect walls, each section perfect and even, on one side each section bearing windows- although they were indeed underground or in some other dimension. Beyond, as he glanced at them, a whirling void filled with stars was turning slowly, shimmering there as though the windows were a portal directly into the galaxy itself.

SICKNESS IN HELL

There was a carpet below his feet, exceptionally lush and soft, and also hot pink, bordered with a fringe that appeared to be made of solid gold threads. A small section of the right hand wall contained a fireplace and several bookshelves, which spanned up all the way to the ceiling about forty feet above. He noted also that in the central panel of the rectangular ceiling, parted from the sides by more mahogany, was a picture of a gigantic penis curling around and devouring itself like an ouroboros, surrounding a globe depicting the planet Earth.

There was a huge mahogany chair, facing away from him, at the end of the room, turned in the other direction. Silence came from the chair and from every other part of this strange chamber, and as he very slowly made his way forwards, he could see the occasional puff of white smoke rise from it, drifting lazily off to the side towards the fireplace.

Halfway across the room, a voice rang out. "Stop."

The chair creaked, and then began to slowly turn, and there, sitting before him not ten yards ahead, was Satan himself, that old serpent. He was gigantic, nine feet tall or thereabouts, and entirely as Germaine had imagined- a thin neck, sallow flesh, leathery wings, squinty, semi-reptilian eyes, the whole shebang. Momentarily afraid of this monumental demon, Germaine was put off in his reaction by the pink, fuzzy slippers Satan was wearing, and the corncob pipe he was smoking. There was a little green bag next to the devilish throne on a little table, and Germaine could smell the demon dank wafting from the purgatory pipe.

"Do you know why you are here?" Satan's voice was hoarse and deep, but there was a second voice, it seemed, behind it, such that it sounded like he was speaking in two tones at the same time; the second, echoing voice he emitted was higher and more feminine.

"I don't know."

"The time has come at last, *you* will bring forth sickness and Hell into the world."

He had no idea what this meant but decided to play along; it wasn't a good idea to perturb demons.

"How did I get here?

"I brought you here. You took quite a knock from that artillery cannon and were almost dead. I had to replace one of your legs." The Devil gestured and Germaine looked down at his left leg, which indeed had been sewn back together with numerous stitches, all of which looked like they were made of the same golden thread as the carpet trim.

"Yes, Germaine, it's gold, only the best for my most valuable acolytes."

"How did you know what I was thinking?

"Never mind that." Satan loaded up his pipe, taking

SICKNESS IN HELL

voluminous time to do so, pinching one of his marijuana
buds in his long, horny fingers, and dusting it into the bowl,
before huffing it all up in one hit, lighting the thing with a
flame which came out of his hand through some magickal
force like a thin tendril of hot vapor.

"Everything every christian ever believed is wrong.
I am lord of this world, god is dead, and the salvation of
man will be the overthrow of all old orders." He spoke
without ever exhaling the hit, then released a cloud of
smoke, smirking there like only a demon can, his lips
thinned and drawn back across hideously projected cheek
bones, high and alien to the biological world itself. "The
infection you have contracted was not my doing I assure
you, but now mankind is in a pickle- I know you don't
realize it, but most of mankind is gone already, and they're
all here with me in Hell. Those people you saw suffering
earlier were not what you would call sinners. Rather, I am
purging them of their fear by desensitizing them. How kind
of me, correct?"

Germaine didn't reply but was distracted by Satan's
hand gestures, as he reached into his loincloth- the only
thing he had on other than his fuzzy slippers, and withdrew
a stash bag larger than the former, hurling the last few
pinches of apparent stem and seed into the fireplace
effortlessly as he proceeded to load another bowl, not
offering any of his demonic chronic to Germaine.

"Mine." He said, hitting it again, exhaling more
quickly.

SICKNESS IN HELL

"I always thought god was good, you were evil, and you wanted people to suffer."

"Oh they do that well enough by themselves, look at your world; what caused the sickness? Greed, stupidity, it's always the same, always has been always will be. But now as you will admit, you're a lot more durable than you were before, yes? You could probably do drugs and it wouldn't kill you, you could get a bad sexual disease and it wouldn't matter. You can kill people and get away with it. I suppose if mankind exists in this condition it will be easier for nature to forgive his mistakes. Maybe, he will make fewer of them, too."

"What do you wish for me to do? Everyone is dead other than a few of us, are you telling me to repopulate? And what about when I die, do I come here? What happens to everyone else?"

"Now now, no more mysteries for today" he wagged his finger at Germaine. "I will tell you more someday, perhaps, but right now what I wish for you to do is bring my forces back into the world, so that I can help you physically. There is an old magick in the world woven by one of my adversaries keeping me out. You can undo this, for the time is finally right for it. I will send you back to the world, right where you left off, and I will kill some of those soldiers that were shooting at you, also, so you can get back to the others. Then, you will use my mark and bring me forth."

It seemed simple enough to Germaine, who was

eager enough to leave Hell and get back to a place more mundane and less ethereal.

"Okay, I'll go back and do this ritual stuff, thing for you."

Satan fidgeted a little bit in his chair and gazed at Germaine with a glazed expression, reaching into his loincloth and playing with himself for a moment, grunting slightly and grinning.

"Very well, you can proceed. A small host will accompany you- it's all I am able to project into the world at the moment, but that will give you the ability to get back through those woods and away from the cannons of the enemy. Be assured that great things are to come in this realm. Now, here you go, this is my mark."

He tossed a small object at Germaine's feet and he picked it up- it was the size of a half dollar, and about as thick, a metal talisman of sorts with a piece of paper glued to the back of it. Neither the paper nor the talisman had any markings on them, and Germaine was confused.

"Wait, what exactly am I supposed to do?"

"The sickness that is spreading is blessed and good; place the talisman on the altar of your little home and soak the paper in some fungus water or something close enough to it and the writing will appear. It is hidden from anyone not aware of this practice. I take no chances, and old habits die hard."

SICKNESS IN HELL

Germaine turned and walked back out of the chamber. The demons inside gave a round of applause and acted like he was the greatest thing they had ever seen in the history of mankind. As he turned for one last look at Satan he could see that the Devil was pleasuring himself and groaning with pleasure, and the doors quickly shut themselves.

The head demon, the one with laughing fits, snapped his fingers and the antechamber dissolved into void around them. Moments later the same treeline Germaine had been ambushed at prior appeared, and the demons swung around, warning him to run for cover as they began charging down the valley at great speed. Momentarily, Germaine stood there, seeing it was still mid day- he didn't realize that it was the day after he had departed originally and figured maybe he had been hallucinating until he saw the Devil's sigil in his hand. His pack was still there next to the dirt crater, scarified and torn apart by the blast, and he whipped around and jogged back through the trees and to the dirt path as the artillery roared behind him and the demons cackled with glee, each one disappearing into thin air as he turned to look behind him.

Not five minutes later down the path he met his visibly exhausted sister, who inquired about his absence.

"Oh boy I have stories for you, Sis."

They departed and made their way back to the citadel without issue.

X. WAR!

By the Germaine and Dawn had returned to the settlement they were all building, it was almost dusk, and the setting sun cast eerie shadows across the yard through the uneven spikes of the inner wall which had been constructed. Bucket by bucket, the dirt had been excavated to a depth of two feet around the blocks adjoining the area, and piled up at the edge of the roads running outside of the miniature city state suggested prior. This difficult task was not even remotely complete, but some progress was better than none, and Germaine held off telling those around him about what had transpired, figuring it might be good to at least reinforce the innermost wall before calling forth hordes of demons which, after all, he had no guarantee of being genuine in their intentions.

All he chose to explain that selfsame night was that he had been knocked out by a field cannon and had thankfully escaped being utterly blown to pieces. Adam was obnoxiously chowing down on a bowl of heavily charred human remains which he had obtained from one of the nearby homes, as he listened, and gave a sideways glance as if to indicate he knew Germaine wasn't telling the whole story.

Over the prior day, a number of corpses had been piled up in the basement of the church- the strange fungus which had infested the processing plant had spread and now there were little hyphae dotting the entire town, especially in wet spots or anywhere where a body had been;

bodily fluids which had soaked through the decaying flesh of so many victims were now overlain by smears of hyphae and tiny mushrooms. On a hunch, Adam had taken some of this infected material and smeared it on a corpse, and the entire cadaver had soon decomposed into a liquefied smear which grew enormous mushroom caps- this he related to the others and, within the same day, an entire farm of tasty fungus was growing in their little citadel.

"I want to get a wood chipper and homogenize some more bodies and make a little garden, maybe under some trees" he said, still chowing down on charred remains. "Probably a good food source for winter."

"How the heck do we know that stuff isn't poisonous?" Dawn was concerned with the idea- mushrooms weren't her forte.

"Well I already ate a bunch of them, I feel fine. Actually, it seems to have miraculous effects."

In truth, Adam did look less sloppy and obese than before and had visibly grown a bit more muscular and less awkward- Germaine didn't know that the fungus was necessarily responsible for this, but he decided to grab a couple handfuls of the stuff anyways from a burlap sack full of fresh mushrooms Adam had harvested and ate a few. He *did* suddenly feel a burst of energy. It also made him feel a little bit light headed, almost high, like it was mildly psychotropic. A warm wave of energy seemingly rippled over his body as the material was digested, and his muscles ached slightly- apparently it stimulated the growth of tissue because he felt like he'd just lifted weights for a good hour straight.

A short night passed with Germaine getting relatively little sleep- becoming unconscious was a little bit frightening to him at the moment because the last time he'd done so he went to Hell.

The next day he decided to at least tell Dawn about his adventure. When he mentioned Satan in pink slippers she worried he'd been severely brain damaged by the blast, but then he showed her the little talisman and she decided that enough strange things had happened that, maybe, she could believe him.

"Well why not do this little ritual thing now and see what happens?"

"I kind of wanted the outer wall to be done first, I wouldn't believe any of it myself if it weren't for the fact that I actually have this in my hand in the first place. What if it was all some sort of evil trick?"

"You eat hobos and we're growing mushrooms on corpses in our basement, Germaine, I wouldn't worry too much."

He didn't very much like this reasoning; she was sort of right, of course, but it made it sound like she thought he was arguably more demented than the Devil, and this seemed like a bit of an insult. Then again, all Satan had done was masturbate in front of him.

SICKNESS IN HELL

"Okay."

They took the little talisman to the main room of the church along with a couple of Adam's mushrooms, leaving the others to their morning routine; Gran was still asleep, sprawled out on one of the benches with a half eaten pie next to her, and Adam was atop the bell tower gazing out over the town. Peter was out getting supplies, his kids left outside with their cat to dig out the little trench that would lay just outside a second wall of debris when finished.

The snoring of Gran sounded an awful lot like a freight train- her fluid filled lungs chortling and vibrating, each exhalation letting loose a little stringer of sticky phlegm down dripping almost to the floor before being inhaled again. Over this ridiculous noise Germaine prepared the altar, clearing off some tools that had been left there, then placing the talisman onto it.

"I'm supposed to soak this in mushroom." He waved the little paper at Dawn and crushed two of the caps up, into a little bit of water from the bucket beside the altar moved to a bowl- a cheap firefighting measure that Adam had helpfully contrived in case of electrical problems from his solar cells. He dipped the paper into the bowl and wiggled it around to get it soaked, then withdrew it and placed it on the altar alongside the talisman.

He didn't have long to wait- writing soon began to manifest itself on the sheet, glowing dimly, perhaps some sort of strange reaction with the fungus itself. Germaine laughed under his breath about a vision appearing in his mind regarding Satan studying chemistry, in his pink slippers, like a middle school nerd dissolving dead insects in nitric acid and pretending to be Doctor Frankenstein.

The instructions were fairly straightforward- place the talisman on the altar, drain a little of his own blood onto it, and then call on Satan with a short Latin invocation.

He tried to slice one of his fingers a little to get blood onto the talisman and no blood came forth; his body was healing too fast for a single drop to fall, and he didn't figure a single drop would be enough anyways, in all likelihood.

He attempted to stab his hand with a screwdriver, working it in and grinding it right between two of his lower finger bones with a sickening rubbery noise as it separated the cartilage there, but as before the only blood was a tiny sheen on the tool itself, the wound dry and quickly regenerating.

"Sis, I think we're going to need a bigger injury."

"What?"

"I can't get any blood. Cut my hand off."

She didn't even change facial expressions. She just stood there, bearing the "you're certifiably a lunatic" look that is usually reserved for people who just said they were going to marry someone they met a week ago.

SICKNESS IN HELL

"I'm not going to ask if you're nuts, because you are- I'm not cutting off your hand."

"Sis, I just impaled myself with a screwdriver and didn't get a drop, either cut my hand off or find a syringe and prepare to go to town."

He chose his words carefully- Dawn was terrified of needles and he knew that she'd sooner lop his head off with a chainsaw and sew herself up inside his scooped-out flesh than even touch a syringe. "I hope your magical spooky dooky healing lets you grow a new hand because I'm not jacking you off as charity."

It took her a few minutes to find the sword, which had been misplaced- for some reason it had been left on one of the benches instead of in the office where it had been intended to stay, ready for use in case of attack. She came back with it already drawn from its little scabbard, and she hesitated again.

"Now, you do understand that I don't like this idea, I oppose it, I deny any responsibility for it, and you're a nut, yes?"

"Just cut my damn hand off. I already regret the idea but it sounds better than slicing my neck and bending over an altar."

"Okie dokie then."

She stood back a few feet from him as he stretched

SICKNESS IN HELL

out his hand right over the talisman, remembering that in all likelihood it was harder to lop his hand off now that he was mutated- she didn't want to miss and take off his face with the hand and told him to bend his face back- he had been half bending over, probably hoping to see the moment his limb was severed. He did, and she brought the sword back, still thinking the entire idea was crazier than anything else she'd seen, and closed her eyes for just a moment before bringing the blade swinging down with the greatest force she could muster.

The razor edge of the blade sliced right through the wrist, severing the digit at the joint, cutting right through the cartilage of the joint, ripping the rubbery stuff in half right down the middle. The sound was sickening; like cutting apart a piece of tire with scissors, a wet, slightly squishy sound. Inside the wrist stump was little else but muscle, except for the bone, which looked diseased and blackened, but a few veins here and there gushed out a little shot of hot blood right before sealing themselves. Indeed, with one now useless hand hitting the altar with a thump and falling to the floor, another began growing from the stump within a half second at most- flesh almost immediately wrapped around the wound and Germaine had barely begun reading the invocation when the thumb began growing out, connected to little dusty hyphae around it- it seemed a sort of strange fungal symbiosis:

> *In nomine inferno,*
> *Et incarnatus est de fungos*
> *solvere et portae inferi*
> *sinistrum et exeunt!*

SICKNESS IN HELL

Nothing appeared to happen. Dawn almost shook her head and went off to steal Gran's pie, but had barely turned around when the building was hit with a jolt like a tremor- not an earthquake, just a jolt, as though a meteor had hit nearby. Another jolt followed, larger than the first, and then things stabilized.

Germaine meanwhile was watching his new hand grow with rapt attention. The digits were fairly steaming with fungal action, some sort of massive metabolic process, and his stomach suddenly felt dreadfully empty. He drained the fungus water and ate all the chunks, devouring it like a shark would a bucket of chum- it took the edge off the gut pain but he'd have to eat something larger soon. As his fingers exploded through their birthing hyphae, a shower of spores and pus shot out of his stump like a shotgun blast and splattered all over the altar, sizzling and steaming there, still hot as Hell itself.

Another jolt, far larger than the others, suddenly knocked them right off their feet.

"Who's at the door!?" Gran had started awake, alarmed at the seismic shuddering, flying off the bench and standing, wobbling sideways with the sudden force, her pie forgotten, toppling off the little stool it was resting on, falling top-first (as pies always will) and sitting there oozing berry juices.

"My pie!" She roared, retrieving it and shoveling it in, as a fourth and final, almighty jolt fairly knocked her down face first in the tasty treat, knocking aeons of dust off the uncleaned rafters of the main hall.

Suddenly all was quiet. Adam came galloping down the tower stairs yelling about volcanoes, and a roaring outside shook the windows as Peter's son came hurling down the road in a pickup, exhaust bellowing from its top as he stalled it moments away from colliding with the inner wall, not even shutting it off as he loped across the front yard into the church, flailing his arms in fear.

The jolts had been replaced by some other noise- and Germaine shouted at them all to be quiet for a minute as he stood there in the near silence, hearing, or rather feeling, a distant vibration. The distant sound of a crack, like that of a cannon, echoed into his ears and he ran up to the tower stairs, taking them three at a time as everyone else either followed as well as they could or went outside to observe for danger.

As he topped the tower and leaned over the railing, looking towards the edge of the county where he'd been ambushed, he got a really nice view of the hellstorm there; a massive wall of smoke and ash was furling out of the ground where, it seemed, a huge chunk of forest had simply vanished, replaced by an enormous and irregularly shaped hole or crater, from which, with the aid of binoculars, he could see was emerging a literal army of beings; indeed, a few puffs of smoke from the hillsides off to the left, where the field cannon had apparently been, camouflaged into the treelines there, showed him what was happening- Hell had really opened up after all and now a legion of demons was fighting with the military or the state guard, or whoever had been stationed there.

With a deafening crack a chunk of rock the size of a skyscraper levitated up from the crater and, as if by magic, hurled itself into the hillside, flattening it and stripping it of vegetation, leaving an enormous swath of destroyed, brown-and-gray rock and dirt behind. The jolt from this massive impact shook the church and the general distant, ambient sound of battle sounded across Hillcrest. It seemed Satan was allied with more than just demons though- there were several large flying beasts and many small, hovering figures whose backs were turned to their position; and Germaine had no idea what these things were. At least one of the flying things looked vaguely like a dragon, except with too many legs- a flying centipede, he presumed.

Dawn grabbed the binoculars and Germaine laughed and praised Satan, because it seemed the demonic horde there was on their side, or at least was opposed to people that had wanted him dead. Dawn was in literal shock and sat down on the floor as Adam took the binoculars in turn and grimaced, having not been told what this legion was or where it came from.

"Think we're about to get flattened by a mountain?" He fiddled with the binoculars and looked like he wanted to flee in the opposite direction, West, perhaps into the mountain chain there further beyond the hills surrounding the county.

"No, those are the 'good' guys." Germaine waved his hands and clenched them in quotations as he spoke, then briefly mentioned the ritual and his visit to Hell to Adam, who scoffed at him and didn't believe such a thing. Peter had finally undulated up the stairs on his deformed abdomen, followed by Gran, who complained first and foremost about the loss of her pie and second about stairs being too steep. Peter couldn't even rear up far enough to glance over the side and Adam related to him what was happening. He made much better time down the stairs than up and shouted that he was going to lock himself in the basement, ignoring Germaine's pleas to listen to reason and not be afraid.

Aided by supernatural speed, a column of demons emerged on the edge of the town and were quickly moving in on their position. Germaine told the others it was fine and he'd go meet with them.

By the time he got down to the inner yard they were speeding across the road right next to the citadel. They were moving their legs like they were walking, but for each step they seemed to move about ten yards- certainly, he knew, it was some sort of diabolical cosmic force aiding them.

"Hello friend, no need to worry about those folks on the hill over there that shot at you, they're dead now." The demon was holding a long wooden pole with a spear on the end on which was impaled the grizzly, dripping face of a soldier, replete with a gas mask, which seemed to be half full of saliva and blood, trickling down the chin slowly, painting the bottom of the metal spear head red and brown with grime.

SICKNESS IN HELL

"We thank you very much for letting us into the world, Satan would like to speak with you again."

With a roar of insane laughter, Satan, now visibly larger than before, came reeling across the lawn from behind one of the homes next to the church. He had his arms up straight in the air and a lunatic grin on his bony face, and his penis appeared to have grown about ten sizes as well- it was spinning around in circles, and Satan was urinating wildly as thought to prepare a path to run on.

Only wearing his slippers and a conical pink hat with a yellow tassel on the top, Satan stood there in the nude before them all, grabbing one of the demons and ripping his head sideways on the spot, ripping it off with a horrific snapping sound as bone, vein, and tendon gave way, pissing on the crumpled, beheaded corpse when he had done so, tossing the head to one of his fellows, who did not have a head already impaled on his pike. With one movement, the demon lowered the weapon, straddling it, holding it up with his knees as he brought the demon head down, spearing it there like a rotting cantaloupe.

"So what happens now? Now that you're free from Hell I mean."

"Free? From Hell? Hell is a nice place, but now we have two nice places, we will of course be sharing it with your race now." Satan bent down and grabbed his enormously long, wrinkly devil dick and reached inside his urethra, pulling out a cigar, which he promptly lit and smoked to the end in one gigantic, incubus inhalation. "We

118

have to prepare this general area. You know there are a lot of mutants out there that aren't as friendly as the people here, Germaine, I'd watch out for them. I have a sort of covenant and I can't help you if you're righting with others who have taken the blessing of the fungus I have given them. I will, though, help you with clearing out some of the retarded people out there."

"You mean the people who haven't gotten fucked up?"

"Fucked up!" Satan bent over laughing and punched the one demon that failed to follow suit in the stomach, sending him and his pike to the ground in agony and paralysis. "You still don't get it my confused, decaying friend, you all have been given immortality. You keep eating and don't get completely mutilated or burned to a crisp and you'll never get sick, you'll never age. Eat rotting piles of garbage if you want, it makes no difference. Man ruined this world, now it will be a cleaner, happier place, interspersed with regions utterly desecrated with a total lack of human order and filled with poison and trash and decrepitude and vestigiality, just like I always wanted!" He chuckled and went silent for a moment, staring at the sky as though deep in thought contemplating the beauty of a post-apocalyptic world filled with hideous mutants and elven gardens of pure color and verdant serenity.

"What should we be doing?"

"Do what you want" Satan responded, "The world is now yours- except what I want for myself. Those hills over there on the other side of the valley will make a nice little vacation spot, but mostly what I mean is subterranean-demon and mutant living side by side, or rather top and bottom, you can be my top any time." He licked his lips and his member was twitching and Germaine grew slightly uncomfortable.

"Are you gay?"

"Omnisexual, I will fuck anything I want."

He reached up and grabbed one of the soldiers' heads and began rubbing it on his nipples and smiled quite warmly, as though Germaine was a very old friend he hadn't seen in decades. "There is too much work to do though" he said "for much enjoyment quite yet. Those hills aren't hollowing themselves out. Oh, and by the way, three bits of advice before I go."

"Fire away."

"First, there are actually a lot of humans who survived intact, and some of them are already aware of your presence and forming militias. I can't defend you until the hills are hollowed out properly so you will need to fortify your position more. Thankfully for you, they're pretty disorganized. Second, your friend up there" he pointed to the bell tower and Adam, who was watching with astonishment, "Is a genius, farm the mushrooms and you will eat well and gain my blessing."

"And third?"

SICKNESS IN HELL

"Third is, there is an old woman living not far from here that you should visit, out in the swamps not too far from the plant, roughly a half mile North of it in fact. I suggest you go speak with her."

"Why would I want to do that?"

"You don't trust Satan's judgment" he said in the third person. "Oh well, I believe you will speak with her, curiosity is so innate to your kind."

He turned and the demonic host planted their heels and spun around in perfect synchronicity, like a British guard unit practicing before the Queen. Before Germaine could utter another word they had already begun storming down the street back towards their crater, as before taking one step for every ten yards of distance, like a spectral host levitating inches above the ground, cushioned by a magickal auric force.

Germaine grinned at Adam when he returned to the church, and told him to expand his mushroom farm at all hazards. He announced that he had to take another, shorter journey.

"This time you're not leaving without me, I don't trust that you'll come back." Dawn was adamant.

With daylight to spare they grabbed the sword and bat and headed out, leaving the others mildly confused but too busy to question the situation.

XI: PICKING UP THE PIECES

Dawn and Germaine had quite a time of walking through the slowly degrading town and into its outer, more rural reaches- it wasn't the fact that little veins of fungus spreading out like toxic roots in the pavement had cracked it apart slightly and made it a bit uneven, nor was it the abnormally hot and humid weather- indeed, their mutated forms compensated for this delightfully well; their pores seemed to have a mind of their own and allowed them to perspire with great efficiency, even if the little barnacle-esque craters dotting their flesh looked hideous and took some time to get used to, since their slow opening and closing drew their skin taut then slackened back to leave it looking rubbery and stretched thin like overcooked pork.

It was Satan's consistent trolling that bothered them most. Groups of demons had begun spilling out of the melee off to the other side of the valley and the beings continually annoyed them, alternately bowing to Germaine like a second Satan and laughing drunkenly in the fringe of the woods, watching them walk and gurgling their alcohol while ranting at the same. Dawn didn't know whether to feel safer because Satan was supposedly their ally or unsafe because the beings were inebriated. Some of them were dimunitive- little more than deformed imps wearing dusty and primitive body armor that resembled something out of the copper age, others were large; some even gigantic. They'd seen more than one lurching ogre or troll lumber through the woods crushing small trees and carrying a backpack full of companions; it seemed this was some sort

SICKNESS IN HELL

of Satanic cavalry, for each of these larger creatures, skin leathery and plated like a rhinoceros, had at least four and usually more of the tiny imps on it, each imp armed with a sort of device that looked like a crossbow with a tommy gun drum attached- a little circular metal thing holding what appeared to be darts or small bolts. Germaine surmised that when the machine was cranked it probably fired them fairly quickly, and he didn't feel like antagonizing any of these creatures and silently hoped they'd keep a distance.

While they made their journey the rest of their kin were simultaneously greeting and attempting to keep track of the demons which had gone AWOL and abandoned the fighting to raid the town of Hillcrest. Some of them had piled dead soldiers in the middle of the street and begun immolating them with kerosene, dancing around in a drunken stupor while others threw rocks through windows haphazardly or passed out from alcohol poisoning. Gran thought these little goblins were absolutely delightful and chased them around cackling and offering them pie; which some of them were sober enough to eat without making a mess. She ended up sitting indian style on the grass in front of their temple surrounded by a group of singing demons which applauded her food and proceeded to have a little party. Their cat meanwhile, was ambivalent towards the trolls and orcs but terrified, for some odd reason, of the tinier sort, and was busy huddling in a tree swishing its decaying tail back and forth and coughing up football-sized hairballs from having devoured a couple of them. Adam and Peter were having a discussion on the oddities they were seeing, and both of them were stoned out of their gourds too- Peter said that the demons showed no real sense of the value of their compatriots, watching and laughing maniacally when the cat had been ripping several of them apart. Peter nodded and then nodded off entirely, drooling phlegm from his puffy mouth and keeling over to the side. Then Adam noticed that, somehow, he'd gotten ahold of what the demons had been drinking- it smelled like rum of a sort; not good, but not strictly poisonous. He tasted the stuff and immediately regretted it- too spicy.

Peter's skeletonous son and charred daughter began taking supplies from the routed soldiers, taking a few trips with the pickup truck, the latter driving and silently considering whether running over demons was allowed. There were a powerful lot of weapons and armor and other goods lying around the crater where the demons had come out from- their numbers had reduced and the distant sound of fighting from behind the nearest line of hills told her that the demonic divisions were still clashing with the military of men; explosions like thunderclaps and the occasional wafting cloud of dirt and smoke ebbed over the hill line, as they tossed the good shit haphazardly into the back of the truck, into the squashed and all-too-small backseat, into the floor of the front, and even stashed in the glove compartment. They had firearms, body armor, medical supplies, canned goods, drums of ammunition (although neither of them knew what ammo went to what guns) and some tents too, which had survived the fighting more or less intact. They even managed to grab a fuel truck with its keys still in the drivers' seat and charred sister commanded her fellow spawn to pilot it; it wasn't full but it wasn't empty.

SICKNESS IN HELL

With such goods requisitioned they felt fairly sure they had enough supplies to put up a good fight against even a well prepared foe. The small field gun hitched to the back of the field truck was the final cherry on the cake- it came with a whole crate of what they, unfamiliar with military hardware, took to be "oversized bullets."

Neither Germaine nor his sister nor anyone else knew where Satan was. They could have gotten quite a show if they had wandered over just the nearest line of hills; for there he was, dressed up in plate armor painted with black and white checker patterns, slowly waltzing through several ranks of terrified soldiers, lopping off heads with a sword deliberately smithed into the crude similitude of a penis, laughing as things burst into flames or exploded around him. He had a host following close behind him blasting disco music on a portable music system too, and in between chopping off peoples' heads he was doing a little dance, something like a true moonwalk, where he literally floated an inch or so off the ground. In his head, Satan wondered if he should stop for a while and consume some of the half-burned and dripping bodies around him, whether demonic or mortal, but kept going, figuring he could pile all the corpses together in a vat and heat them and then go swimming in their rendered fatty remains.

The small home that Dawn and Germaine happened upon, right where Satan had said it would be, was overgrown and shabby- it probably didn't look good even before the disaster. They had no idea exactly what they were meant to do, and Dawn was getting spooked by the property itself; dark, filled with twisted trees in various states of dilapidation, mostly dying, some already dead, a few verdant but overgrown and obviously left to their own devices, stretching their branches through the dying understory of their compatriots to the sun above to gain what sustenance they were able to gain.

The home itself was aesthetically pleasing, or would have been if half the paint wasn't chipping loose and the clay tiles of the roof weren't crumbling slowly, leaving a discolored fringe underneath the drip line where decaying sediment from the reddish clay was staining the dying grass below a sort of rusty color. Though small, it looked quite long- not a shotgun row home, a ranch style dwelling with what had once been a nice raised cement base and light blue painted siding. It had the typical wider-than-tall ranch home windows too, which Germaine thought pleasing and Dawn thought abominable.

A crash from the building told them someone was home, which was fortuitous but also regrettable at the same time- Satan could claim it was a grand idea to talk to the owner but neither of them truly wanted to do so.

They inspected one of the front windows and saw nothing but dimness inside- whoever was there had lit a few lanterns and they cast the faintest reddish light across the interior of the living room, casting shadows on the wall not resembling the vases and piles of papers they were actually projecting. Another crash sounded off to the back of the home and they approached the rear, observing there a large pile of refuse and garbage which was shivering and moving.

SICKNESS IN HELL

"You okay?" Dawn stepped to the side to get a better view but it was not immediately apparent what was actually there. Germaine stood at the very corner, ready to bludgeon whatever it was if it wasn't friendly. He was glad he had stood back, because one of those trash bags suddenly got tossed to the side where he would have likely been standing, and a whole festival of life came surging out of the rancid pile of garbage- a pair of raccoons, and a tidal wave of what appeared to be mutated termites, swollen and smelly, having gorged themselves on waste. Dawn reeled back as the raccoons, fat and happy off their termite meal (and apparently not mutated at all) trudged off between her legs and into the woods, ignoring them both, and the swarm of bugs skittered around making squishy "bugs in the trash" sounds. She lost her lunch all over the ground and the termites immediately began eating her vomit, churning through it and slopping the hideous pile up into their squishy little bug bodies, and she lurched into the treeline, further from them, before puking again.

This was mildly amusing but Germaine didn't get to chuckle for long as a sallow hand came down- hard- on his left shoulder. He turned instantly, and was looking into the face of a woman so old she might have been his great grandmother, or perhaps the Crypt Keeper. She stared at him with absolutely no expression at all, and then lifted her mouth up in a shit eating grin, bringing out line after line of wrinkles which seemed to emerge like sorcery and decorated her entire face- from scalp to neck there was nothing but a grinning wrinkle, each small ridge in her skin forming a colony of the same.

SICKNESS IN HELL

"Ya scared off my coons." The woman wheezed and slapped her knees and threw one fist to the sky, appearing at least to have been driven insane.

"Sorry."

"Don't be sorry I hate the bastards." She reached into her pocket and fiddled around and withdrew what Germaine thought looked like half a dead rat, and stuffed the raw morsel of flesh into her mouth, which still contained maybe half of her teeth, and tore out a chunk, hair and all, squeezing what remained over her face and leaking blood into it, accidentally getting some rodent hemoglobin in her eye and wiping it away, leaving a stain there along her left cheek.

"I suppose that old serpent sent you."

Dawn had returned from the edge of the woods, a spattering of puke still dotting the front of her shirt. "How the heck did you know that?" She was disgusted at the rat hair speckling the woman's face like a sparse beard but she had given no indication of malice.

"Oh I used to fuck him when I was younger, used to rail his cock up inside me every weekend. Even when I was married!" She cackled and grabbed her crotch, which even through her skirt appeared to be dangling somewhere down between its normal location and her knees. Dawn cringed and backed away a little bit. "Oh don't worry we used protection, no chance of demon spawn." With a laughing fit working its way to her verbal surface, the old woman began

SICKNESS IN HELL

hacking and spat out a chunk of rat hair.

"Satan is the greatest maker of mischief in creation." She said, suddenly stern and clasping her hands like a bored professor. "I suggest you plan for the inevitable day that he decides to randomly off all of you."

"Don't we have a sort of pact though? He doesn't appreciate us?" Germaine was confused.

"Oh deary of course he does." She smiled in an unmistakably genuine manner and cocked her head down slightly to the side. "He just has... issues. Don't worry though if you die I suppose you can just be in Hell. Everyone goes to Hell, but the real trick is that there is no god and the poor boy gets so lonely, he just wants people to disco with him and get him off, you know, people that aren't deformed or drunk all the time. His demons give him so much angst."

Dawn cleared her throat and gave Germaine a look that could only mean "she's batshit." Germaine rolled his eyes at little sis and continued to question her. "So why would he send us to you if he planned to slaughter us too? Why would he warn us beforehand?"

She laughed maniacally and opened her eyes so wide that they bulged out to Graves-disease levels. "Because he likes the sport of it! He wants you to fight back." She calmed down and gave him a knowing look. "And if you win, oh boy good things to come. I can help you there..."

SICKNESS IN HELL

The conversation that ensued lasted for only a few minutes. The woman was nuts, but she was skilled in magic and told them she could prove it- with a flick of her wrist she sent loose a blast of fire from her hand and immolated her entire property, sending the trees up so quickly that the carbon was left behind from their searing flesh, leaving behind, for a moment, trees made entirely of charcoal, which quickly fell apart under their own weight and came down into loose piles which tinkled together like the clink of pennies as the metallic clumps bumped and jolted against each other like falling pillars of salt.

She flicked it again. The termites swarming at their feet suddenly died. Another flick and they levitated into the air, then all smashed together, then were briefly surrounded by a sort of reddish halo before the blob of bug flesh stretched out into the semblance of a cobra and reanimated itself almost instantly and slithered off to the front of the home, apparently opening the door by itself and letting itself in.

"I can do a lot of things, I've been doing this for a long time. But now, you have a home to defend; those mutated freaks Satan warned you about are approaching, and will present themselves at dawn. I suggest you hop along home for now, and I will enjoin you in battle when Satan tries to test you all. Honestly, I don't think he knows how powerful I have become in my necromantic ways, or he probably wouldn't have dared send you to little old me." She laughed again, and her other pocket soon produced a second morsel for her; a little bag that she opened, pulling out what looked to be eyeballs, maybe human, maybe canine- she chewed right into them and a spray of eye fluid came squirting out, hitting Germaine in the face.

"Now go!" She threw up her hands and began cackling with insanity, dancing around and flailing her arms and casting spells in random directions, sending fireballs into the woods where they exploded into roaring fires along the trunks and brush they impacted with. And some sort of energy came shooting out of her mouth and hit the dead willow in front of her home, after which the plant groaned, shook, shuddered, and began tearing its own roots from the earth like it was alive and possessed of conscious capabilities. Germaine took Dawn's hand and booked it back down the road leaving the mad woman behind, screeching and briefly chasing them, holding up her skirt and exposing her dangling labia, which swayed to and fro beneath her, slapping her against her knees and staining them with piss.

As they jogged back, Dawn warned Germaine it was a terrible idea to tell the others most of what they had just seen and heard; they'd get curious maybe and want to see the crazy witch themselves, and they might grow despondent at the idea that the work they were doing would probably be crushed by a legion of demons. He agreed; but they needed to tell the others to expect an attack in the morning and to prepare.

XII: RELATIONS TURN SOUR

The happy family began working feverishly as soon as Germaine told them that attackers were on their way. By the late afternoon they had erected a primitive series of spikes and debris along the half complete embankment they'd constructed, predominantly to slow any attacker down while they fired on them- it almost seemed superfluous, though, since they had a field gun mounted atop a simple cinderblock-and-plank platform on a sort of little hill where a rich bitches' grave used to sit- shoring it up and filling it in more or less flat to make a yard-high little tower was simple. With all the weapons they'd pilfered (only two of which failed to fire and had apparently been damaged by fighting) each one of them had enough ammunition to stave off a horde.

The demons which had been so prevalent had begun to filter back over the hills- only a few stragglers now remained in the area, a few that were heavily inebriated and incapable of walking, a few that were asleep, and one which had eaten some of their fungus and mutated horribly, turning into a sort of half-demon half-spider being which was making clicking noises and building a web on the bell tower. Incapable of conversation, the hideous being simply sat there glowering at the rest of them, but was being tolerated for its apparent disinterest in attacking.

The body armor turned out to be mostly useless. Mutated as they were, only a few bits of the same kevlar sets even fit their bodies. Germaine managed to squeeze a plate carrier on but it barely reached his midriff, and most of them (other than Adam with the pinhead) had combat helmets- most of the rest of the armor was cast aside into the debris pile with the rest of the trash. Gran cooked up a terrific idea, though, and the result was frighteningly strong.

She took some of the plates and began padding their cat with them- bolting the same together until the miniature sabertooth was covered in what resembled medieval plate armor. A couple of straps below held the contraption on, and soon they had the mutant version of a lightly armored tank roving around in the graveyard, still occasionally prowling about for imps. Unfortunately, Germaine remembered that big kitty was a "fraidy cat" around some life forms and might bolt at any time, perhaps taking a chunk out of their wall with it.

It didn't take long for them to come under attack either. Adam and Dawn were making small talk next to the field gun and Germaine was on the front steps behind a couple of fuel barrels holding an M16 in one hand and a donut in the other when he heard a chattering, laughing, riotous noise from across town, maybe three blocks in the other direction. Everyone perked up at roughly the same time; including the cat and half-deaf Gran. It was funny to see her there holding a stick with a bayonet duct-taped to the end like a pike, combat helmet fitting improperly, tilted back as she sat there grinning and peering over the barrier, cracking jokes about the Atomic Holocaust.

The first foe that emerged wasn't so bad. Much like

the priest they had sparred with many days ago, it was clearly insane, and shaking and shivering and quivering as it lurched around randomly before spotting Germaine, after which it reared back and made a sort of half-gasp, half-laugh noise and began running with its arms straight out at its sides like an Olympic sprinter just about to cross the finish line. Germaine leveled and fired a burst off, sending a spray of bullets through its chest, which blasted two holes in it and caused the being to fall down- its legs kept running and its upper body got jolted backwards, clotheslining him right to the ground. It got up and spat out blood, but a second burst blew its skull clean open and left it twitching.

A second freak, this time with an extra leg hanging out like a tail right above the asshole, made its way on much the same course, its slightly blue flesh almost glowing in the dusky sunlight, eyes bulging out. This time Dawn fired the killing shot, from closer range with a combat shotgun. When the spray hit the freak in the head, the pressure shot both of its eyeballs clean out of its head and emptied the skull entirely, leaving jellied piles of brain all over the barrier and spraying Dawn's front with blood. She reached through and grabbed one of the loose eyeballs and chomped it right down, hungering for flesh, chewing it in half before sucking the eye fluids out.

"Looks like we're prepared a little too well, this is stupid." Adam was getting bored. He had spent all day dreaming of hand to hand open combat and throttling his enemies before stabbing out their guts with a rusty butter knife. "I thought this was supposed to be a well prepared assault, these are just mindless zombies."

SICKNESS IN HELL

Germaine was actually getting a little bit nervous. Satan and the old Necromancer woman had both indicated that they would be attacked by a group, and that required organization, and that required brains, and these freaks didn't have working brains. He put two and two together and decided that somewhere, someone was probably watching the skirmishes they just had, and was plotting the best way to assault them.

It didn't take long for his concerns to manifest physically. The first they heard was a sound like an earthquake, and then they saw, in the dim sunlight, aided slightly by the rays of a full moon, a massive explosion from a street or two behind the row of homes closest to the churchyard. In front of them, several dozen freaks suddenly began ambling at various gaits towards their front, while something large and very noisy approached from the other side.

A vanguard of additional freaks entered their view on that side too- perhaps a dozen more of them, variously mutated and all invariably mindless. Some were missing limbs, all were missing a coherent mentality, all of them were hungry. The field gun roared once and one of them was basically vaporized, the freak behind this poor victim taking the ordinance in the stomach and losing most of its organs. This didn't stop it from attacking- it didn't even bleed.

Germaine, Dawn, and Peter all opened fire. Charred girl and spindly man were inside of the church on the second floor to provide covering fire in case anything broke through. The cat was busy licking its asshole and not helping. Gran was doing the same and cackling in a moment of temporary dementia.

Adam was a good shot- Peter couldn't hit the broad side of a barn. Germaine was somewhere between the two, being more of a blade aficionado. He was worried that Peter might accidentally shoot someone friendly and yelled to him to get to the field gun and use that instead. Relieved of the platform, Dawn grabbed his rifle and switched it to automatic fire, being unsatisfied with dropping them one at a time. She wasted all her ammo but managed to take the legs off of a couple of the approaching horde.

With a monumental blast, a home off to the side where the roaring noise was approaching suddenly collapsed with a cloud of dust. It was then that Germaine instantly recognized the mastermind of the attack- it was Pillwaff, back for revenge apparently, only it was Pillwaff even more hideously deranged than before. She was enormous- an undulating pile of leathery, charred flesh twenty feet tall, and fatter than a Sumo wrestler in every way, her arms like bloated tree trunks, her legs all but fused together into a sort of slug-like pod, which she had somehow hoisted onto a dump truck- not the normal kind that comes around to grab your refuse or deliver a couple tons of gravel for your driveway- one of the big ones, the gigantic kind that gets used in mining operations and can hold ten tons of debris in a load without a problem. With this veil of metal surrounding most of her lower body, the crazy woman advanced, at an extremely slow but steady pace, crushing everything in her path, including one of her

SICKNESS IN HELL

own apparent foot soldiers.

Someone was driving other than Pillwaff herself, she was too busy belching out waves of phlegm, which had dried onto her naked chest, replete with three different pairs of titties, mottled and covered in bruises, each nipple feeding some sort of abomination which she probably herself gave birth to in the days before- these beings were probably about the size of a dishwasher, or so it seemed from what Germaine could see- roughly round, but covered in little legs or tentacles, clinging to her chest and suckling her like the mother of all whores in Babylon.

The driver, as the vehicle steamrolled the earth on its course and grew closer, was apparently a former employee, or so the familiar coveralls of the Hillcrest Plant it was wearing indicated. The front end of the dump truck had also been armored further- plates of scrap metal were bolted mostly haphazardly to it, along with rolls of barbed wire. It was belching nearly black smoke as it moved, and Pillwaff grasped something from the bed of the truck- a rock the size of a basketball- and hurled it at the church, taking a chunk out of it.

A dozen of the mutants managed to get into the enclosure and soon all was mayhem. Charred sis and spindly man popped off bullets into them and dropped one, but soon they couldn't actually provide covering fire as planned, since Adam, Germaine, Dawn, and Gran were all in proximity to the horde, battering them with melee weapons.

SICKNESS IN HELL

Their pet cat had leaped over the enclosure barrier and was dining on one of the attacking freaks while swishing its tail around merrily, ignoring the fighting and glad it had "helped" with this modest contribution. Charred sis and spindly boy soon came rushing out of the church, abandoning their posts, the former immediately smashing an ax into the back of the head of one attacker, splitting its head to the collar bone and killing it instantly, while the latter grabbed one freak, lifted it straight off the ground, and took a knife to the leg from another before sending them both into the debris pile, before blasting them with six shots from his pistol.

The mindless freaks outnumbered them three to one but were terrible at fighting. Germaine was more worried about Pillwaff, who stood atop the dump truck yelling obscenities through lungs full of flesh and soon stopped to grab each abomination in turn off of her nipples, tossing them into the fray. The first latched onto one of the attacking freaks and sucked its hand into its mouth, which Dawn noted looked like that of a lamprey- the oozing maw extended around the hand, then sucked the creature deeper onto the limb, serrating and vampirizing it and twisting to the side using its tentacles, spinning the freak to the ground with a snap of its arm bones, sucking away at its fluids. Even though the being was mad, its face twisted into a semblance of agonizing pain and fear, and it roared and flailed. Dawn took pity on it and blew its head off before firing at the abomination, which responded by apparently becoming malleable, the flesh simply re-sealing around the bullet hole left behind.

SICKNESS IN HELL

She ran at top speed back into the church as Pillwaff emptied her abominations into the fray. More attackers were filing out of the streets too, but the abominations seemed as likely to go after the attackers as their actual enemies, and he was too busy trying to avoid being devoured to care about their presence- the zombies, after all, were more numerous.

Pillwaff grabbed another small boulder and hurled it into the church again, this time impacting the bell tower. She might have thought twice about this, since the entire tower broke off, sending it to the ground right on top of one of her offspring. This managed to do what a bullet couldn't and speared it with splinters of broken oak plank, causing it to leak profusely- the mix inside smelled like rotting potatoes, foul and shitty, like the sediment left behind in a recently drained, poorly maintained pond being heated and baked by the sun. It made Germaine gag, but Adam kept right up, smashing a dagger through the chest of one mutant and using the corpse as a sort of shield, forcing a second attacker into the barrier and shoving until the blade pierced the zombie behind the one already stabbed. He withdrew the same and began slicing off both of their heads, pounding them with the other hand so that they couldn't respond. Blood was caking his face and he was grimacing with a mixture of lust for carnage and merriness.

Germaine took advantage of the fact that the two mutants closest to him were mortally wounded to level his sights on Pillwaff and began spraying her with bullets. Most of them did little, simply lodging in her voluminous fatty tissues, but he did manage to hit her in the left eye, causing her to almost fall off the dump truck. The driver opened the door and responded in kind, sending bullets in his direction. As he fell to the ground to avoid being killed, he saw first one mutant drop, and a second lose its right arm as the rounds exploded through the gristle of its shoulder. A second later, Adam managed to take a hit to the back of his neck and dropped almost instantly, paralyzed as his throat burst open, its viscera spilling out all over the freak he had most recently stabbed and ripped already half apart.

With Adam lurching forwards and slumping down over a dying freak, Germaine returned fire now at the driver, and managed to force them to get back into the truck, which started rolling forwards. He retreated to the steps of the church, where he believed the truck would be unable to follow, as Peter, Gran, and Charred Sis beat their way to the field gun. Spindly boy was crouching behind the barrier sporadically firing into the freaks, dropping another one.

The entire area was now a field of carnage, with one abomination dead under the remains of the fallen bell tower, three of them wandering aimlessly, apparently not hungry, and two of them leeching a dead mutant at the same time, apparently sucking its fluids back and forth through its entire body, each one of them being frustrated by the efforts of the other, each one incapable of resisting the continued urge to feed.

Dawn emerged again, this time with her flamethrower, apologizing and yelling something about refueling as she ran past Germaine, immediately spraying the abominations and roasting them. Filled with decrepit gas as they apparently were, the flames almost immediately caused them to explode in a showering blast of hot guts. The explosion of the first was like a cannon. She immolated the bell tower remains just to be sure and sprayed, a moment later, the front end of the dump truck as well. Unable to see out the front end, the driver abandoned ship and ran off in the other direction almost at the same time that the fire rose to the top end of the front side itself. Germaine emptied his bullets into the fleeing driver and dropped them, intent on finding out who had probably killed Adam.

Without a driver Pillwaff was now stranded and the number of mutants around the yard was decreasing by the second. She resorted to hurling another rock towards Dawn, but missed by a good distance, her visual depth hindered by the loss of one of her eyes. Half blind, she roared as fire began to engulf the paint on the truck, and Dawn sprayed more fire underneath the entire length, then turned and blasted the abominations which had been taking turns sucking the dead fluids out of their shared fallen mutant.

The hideous slug woman began to melt visibly; waving her arms around as her enormous pulsating guts churned with pain. She screeched obscenities the entire time, each word incapable of being understood, then reared back and flopped off of the loader, backwards, falling on a tree stump and impaling herself on the left arm, still flailing helplessly.

SICKNESS IN HELL

Only one of the abominations was still present and Germaine thought it a good idea to punish this wicked old woman for what she had tried to do. The fact that Adam was probably dead or at least paralyzed was bothering him, and he had a little bit of bloodlust coursing through his brain at the moment. He smashed his way through the only mutant left standing and battered it to the ground, leaving only a bloody smear behind where its head used to be, smashed in flat by the butt of his rifle. When he reached Dawn, who was gazing around looking for things to immolate, he disarmed her immediately, and told her he wanted Pillwaff for himself.

Formerly lit rather dimly in the dusky light, a dusk that had finally set behind the trees, the blazing wreckage of the dump truck as the front end was engulfed entirely was more than sufficient for his task. Germaine grabbed the spinal cord of one mutant which had gotten blasted with the field gun and ran over to the last abomination, wrapping the bones around it and squeezing, trying to keep from being leeched by the disgusting thing. It sucked at the bones instead, and because it was distracted and blind, posed no threat as he dragged it over to the impaled Pillwaff, who thrashed around but was too enormous to move ably.

Then he beat the feign around the face and grabbed ahold of her lower jaw, ordering his sister to hold the upper jaw still, cracking the jaw loose, letting out a spray of blood. The bone underneath and the connective tissue was mostly rotting away, crumbly like feta cheese, which pulsed forth from the ruined cartilage and tissue, as he pushed the last abomination into her mouth and began stomping it down spine and all into Pillwaff's throat. She gagged, reaching up to dislodge it, unable to do so because she couldn't get her arm around all of her fat- one of her gigantic breasts was half covering the mutated arm, and pinned it down as Dawn smashed the woman in the nipple with a knife, sending a dribble of rancid cottage cheese clot down her naked, mottled chest.

The flammable creature being lodged firmly in Pillwaff's head, he took up the flamethrower and blasted the abomination, and sure enough within only a few seconds the thing exploded with the force of a hand grenade, blowing the top of Pillwaff's head clean off. The hideous pile of blubber shook, spasmed, and then stood still, laying there dripping.

No foes left to conquer, Dawn hurried her way back into the church to check up on the damage, while Germaine told the others to pile the corpses in the debris barricades to help buff them up. The truck was still burning and proved a hindrance to this plan, since it was close enough to the East side of the debris wall so that it could not, at present, be repaired. The solution was simple, involving a quick flip of a switch to bring the truck's massive metallic back bucket into an upright position, pushing it past the dying Pillwaff to form a barrier of its own where the hole it had made once stood.

Reduced back to boredom, Peter was poking at the giant corpse and not helping his spawn repair the barricades. Germaine was too busy checking up on Adam, or what he believed was probably Adam's corpse.

SICKNESS IN HELL

Indeed, his friend had died- it looked like his fungal colonies had attempted and failed to repair his body, for the damage had been much more severe than just a shot to the neck- the bullet had ricocheted upwards and blown off the top frontal lobe entirely and he had taken a couple more bullets in the melee at some point too. Two holes in his lower back showed Germaine the extent of the physical trauma.

He dragged the corpse into the church and laid it on the altar, mindful that at any time they would face a second, likely worse assault. Without their only substantially good marksman they stood a bit less of a chance.

The attack didn't come until the morning, however- that night none of them slept save the cat, which was bloated after having mostly consumed the exploded guts of the abominations lying around the yard- the mutants had been piled in the barricades but the random sloppy piles of viscera were only of use as food. The happy feline reposed on the front steps of the church and farted at regular intervals as though making a sort of smelly smoke signal, its asshole opening and closing visibly like that of a shitting cow as Germaine sat beside it, gun loaded and ready to go.

The first indicator was a single demonic imp which ran up the street towards them. Dawn was ready to fire on it but thought better of such an act, watching as it simply stood there about ten feet in front of the barricade and exposed its genitals to them, taking a piss on the wooden spokes sticking out at odd angles before running back off cackling like a lunatic.

SICKNESS IN HELL

They didn't have to wait long before a vanguard of goblins arrived- a half dozen of them, each armed only with wooden pikes sharpened on the end to a point. Each of the creatures was perhaps five feet in height and mottled, discolored, and deformed. Hunched over, like they were about to tend the bells of Notre Dame. Germaine fired first, dropping two of them- the bullet piercing the first through the chest and headed on its course right through the pitifully thin armor protecting the being to smash into the thigh of the next in line, which winced and knelt, then bent over sideways. Peter managed to finally hit something and sprayed the rest of them down, laughing the entire time, drool caking his foul purple lips as he waddled forwards on his perch, where he had arranged some debris around the gaping hole in the side of the church and set up a sort of snipers' nest.

"This can't be all of them, I half expect a thousand of them to march on us." Dawn was nervous but Germaine less so- truthfully, it looked like Satan's troops rarely had anything that could kill at a distance, most of the demons he'd seen had nothing less primitive than a broadsword and eve that was a rarity, some of them didn't have any weapons at all, and their armor didn't stop bullets.

A rustling in the trees to their South drew the attention of everyone but Gran, who had cracked open a crate of grenades and was sitting there in a combat helmet and nothing else, masturbating with one of them and grinning as she jerked off their pet cat in a moment of near-divine dementia. They tried their best not to watch this spectacle.

SICKNESS IN HELL

In a moment, two of what they had deemed, loosely, trolls, stepped out of the trees there, still unarmored and still confused and slow, lumbering in their general direction. One of them stopped momentarily and looked around as though it didn't know what it was supposed to be doing, then got smacked in the face by the other, which was carrying a sort of weapon comprised of a leather wrap on its right hand, to which was attached a dome shaped iron club of sorts, only without a handle. Refuted for its mental slowness, the other troll snapped to and continued with its compatriot. This time, bullets did little, but charred sis let loose a shot from the field gun and managed to hit one of them in the stomach, blasting a hole in it there the size of a basketball. Roaring in pain, the being didn't stagger or retreat, but threw its hands up, charged past its fellow troll, and headlong into the barricade.

Flinging dead mutants, wooden poles, rocks, and clumps of dirt around aimlessly, the demonic denizen appeared to be searching for something, then stopped, bent down despite sporadic fire from Peter's nest above, and grabbed a huge clot of turf, stuffing the thing into the cavity left behind where it had been injured. With the wound apparently "fixed" to the mind of this monstrous being, it brought back its left arm and advanced on the field gun as a second shot failed to land, whizzing past its head and exploding behind it, impacting a home there and blasting the corner of the roof loose. It brought the arm down, smashing the barrel as charred sis retreated behind the church, leaving spindly boy to fend for himself.

This he did ably. With the agility of a ninja and the

strength of a barbarian warrior, he grabbed the decapitated barrel and smashed the troll around the side of the head when it stooped over to clutch its stomach in a moment of pain, sending its head sideways and causing it to fall over the little embankment, reeling. Its comrade in arms wasn't pleased seeing his friend injured like this and let out a scream which was something between the howl of a wolf and the high pitched whine of a poorly tuned television set, then hurled a rock in that direction, which didn't hit spindly boy but forced him to duck behind the ruined gun.

Up the street then came a whole column of demons; these looked about the same as before, each of them carrying their spear or ax or sword, all lightly armored, chattering and singing random ditties about fire and drinking liquor. Everyone opened fire at once on them, felling them as they marched, apparently refusing to break rank or charge at full speed. The troll on the ground was now useless and laid there gasping as the other, perhaps slightly more self aware troll, clutched its hand-mace and began swinging it to and fro, slowly walking towards the church. It began attempting to clamber up the wall to reach Peter, and was having some degree of success when Gran stopped beating off her engorged genitals long enough to toss a grenade in that direction. The thing blew up right between the troll's knees and instantly stopped its movement. It stood there, in the same position as it had before the blast, then screamed and reached down to fondle itself, falling backwards off the wall in terror and pain. It managed to scramble to its feet and plowed off back down the road, right through the demons, crashing through them and throwing them to the side with one hand, still holding his damaged genitalia with the other. Five rows back, the demons quickly closed their ranks and began stabbing the beast, one of them managing to work a pike into its eye, through to its brain, as bullets continued to blast the occasional demon into the netherworld.

Gran then took to lobbing the grenades into this column of hideous spawn, each explosion felling three or four of them. Peppered by gunfire and grenades, they continued, marching over their own dead, oblivious, it seemed, to the carnage around them. One saw its fellow demon's face blown off, and the mutilated marcher turned and gurgled at him. This was so uproarious that its fellow hobgoblin bent over double, laughing like a hyena, until the demon behind him stabbed him in the ass to keep him marching.

Dawn grabbed up her flamethrower yet again and began to blast the road in front of them, creating a barrier to their march. They responded by very slowly reorganizing their column and moving to the side. She blasted the turf in front of them again, and the beings, confused, actually huddled together to decide what to do.

While bullets continued to rain down on the ineffectual army, one demon, a grisly head taller than the rest and marked with a red feather in his helmet, told them that maybe they should try something different. He grabbed the nearest demon and slashed his throat, then tossed him into the fire. Others did the same, and after some struggling they literally began to pave a road of corpses on top of the wall of fire in front of them, slowly continuing to march.

SICKNESS IN HELL

Dawn, with only a little fuel left to use, had to make do with immolating a few ranks as the rest continued.

Germaine quickly thought of an idea. He leaped up and grabbed a machete and beckoned to spindly bro and Dawn. Charred sis, looking at the fight from behind the church, took up a position to the side of the debris barricade and continued to pelt the oncoming ranks.

Germaine, his sister, and spindly bro all began to spray automatic fire into the oncoming demonic horde as they marched across the wall of fire Dawn had laid down for them. Their bullets tore through the ranks with great speed, leaving little of the first four rows behind other than blood and dismembered limbs. Germaine took up the machete and, standing in the gap in the fire where they were marching through, began hacking and slashing at them, holding up a piece of armor from one of the corpses on his left hand in front of him like a shield, to take any oncoming blows.

Dawn and spindly bro got the idea. Soon the three of them were fending off an advancing row five demons wide where they had stanched the flames. Funneled into this melee assault, the demons were no match, and with the middle of the column continuously fired on and hit with grenades, their numbers began to wane.

After ten minutes, and a few injuries to Germaine, who took a spear in the right forearm and quickly recovered by gnawing on a chunk of demon flesh, and took a slash to the stomach and didn't have time to do the same for that wound, the demons finally broke ranks and the remainder of the great host fled. A quick estimate of the death toll stood at about four hundred- about half of those which had tried to invade their land.

Germaine let out a cheer, and almost danced with happiness- maybe now Satan would leave them alone. He was let down in this hopeful ideation however, when he heard someone else cheering. It was Satan, and it was a sight to behold.

There, before them, sauntering out of the wreckage of the same house that was missing half of its roof courtesy of the now-defunct field gun, was Satan incarnate. He looked much as he had before, Germaine noted, save for his manner of dress and one particular physical characteristic.

He was wearing a checkered suit- black and white, like a wrap-around chessboard, and a tophat as well. A single demon accompanied him, winged and pale and taller than Satan, holding a disco ball on a string attached to a pike before him, wearing only a tee shirt that said "Satan's bitch." Satan's penis had either grown or Germaine was imagining things- his pendulous balls dragged the ground and the erection he had was longer than his own forearms.

"Good job my pussies and penises." He said, chortling. "Oh also this is Astaroth, he's my wife."

Astaroth didn't look happy, in fact he looked miserable, holding the disco ball as Satan reached over to finger his asshole a little bit, grinning like a car salesman

SICKNESS IN HELL

talking a young couple into buying a lemon. "You drove back my demons, but behold, you can't drive me back."

The devil did something then that seemed even more incredible than anything Germaine had witnessed prior- he fiddled with the tip of his penis for a moment and grunted, then pulled open his urethral opening and pushed two fingers inside the hole, pulling out what looked like a wooden rod, perhaps two and a half feet long. With this wooden instrument removed, his formerly erect phallus drooped to the ground, and Satan had to pick the dripping member up and stuff it inside of his suit, leaving just the tip dangling out, leaking a little bit of urine.

The devil daddy began swaggering slowly towards them all, removing a cigar from one of his shirt pockets and stopping to lazily light it, puffing away on it. Germaine tried to hold him back but spindly bro was ready for combat and lurched ahead to meet him, as Satan chuckled. He stood there, waiting for spindly bro, and as the latter brought back the ruined end of the field gun- an imposing club- Satan brought back his stick and whacked the slender form of his adversary up into his stomach. What looked to be a physically unimpressive strike sent spindly bro flying fifteen feet backwards, and he smashed into the debris pile, laying there looking dazed but largely unharmed.

"Naughty boys get a whacking, oh yeah, oh yes, yesssss, I will whack off." Satan withdrew his penis and yanked it right out leaving only a stump behind, brandishing it like a whip. All things considered he looked a bit like a cocaine addled lion tamer.

SICKNESS IN HELL

Peter fired a shot and hit Satan in the chest. The blow caused him to move to the side, grunting, but it didn't injure him at all. He picked up a rock perhaps the size of a tangerine and tossed it up into the air, smashing it with his stick, and sent the thing speeding off in Peter's direction, hitting not Peter but rather the exposed rafter above him, the plank cracking loose and slapping down under pressure right into his face, leaving a large red bruise behind and breaking his nose. Blood sprayed from both nostrils and he dropped his gun to fondle it.

"I don't have time for you, fat boy." Satan chuckled. "Who else wants to be emotionally abused?"

Dawn didn't have any fire left to deliver, and thinking to herself, she didn't think fire was likely to hurt Satan anyways. She brandished a bayonet in each hand, wielding them like a ninja, walking forwards with each of them drawn across herself in front to guard from any attack.

"Feisty females are almost as good as gay men" Satan quipped, "But your vaginas will never feel as good as a rancid corpse asshole along my virulent venereal villa." He stood back and held his detached penis, then whipped it forwards when Dawn was in range, snapping it at her feet, the member extending as though with a magical capability, the three foot phallus rapidly increasing in length until it seemed to be fifteen feet long. She stood there and hurled one bayonet like a throwing knife, managing to lodge it in Satan's shoulder, but he pulled it out, leaving no evidence of a wound, and hurled it back, shaving off a chunk of

SICKNESS IN HELL

Dawn's scalp in the process. She ran at him with the other blade but he just grabbed her wrist and twisted, causing her to crumple in pain. He kicked her aside and continued.

"Boring people in a boring world, that's why the human race is going to go extinct. I had hoped better for your mentality."

Germaine didn't intend to engage Satan in combat, it was fairly clear he wouldn't prevail. "Why are you attacking us? I thought we were allies?"

"Of course you are little man, and this is how I treat my friends. Watch."

With a wave of his knobby hand he levitated some rocks into place and waved the same again, and soon in front of Germaine was an immaculate but irregular statue of a giant penis standing there where some graves used to be. "I am the end all be all. I want to truncate your colon, Germaine." He grinned and licked his lips. It seemed that Germaine could only survive this by getting his shitter shattered.

But then Satan was taken by surprise. The troll laying by the field gun, which had been staggered last night and left for dead or in a coma, roared and lunged across the embankment right into Satan, grabbing him and tossing him like a rag doll into the street. Visibly terrified, Satan screamed like a woman and tried to crawl towards Astaroth, but Astaroth was laughing maniacally and began to toss clumps of dirt at him as the troll, enraged, grabbed Satan's penis from his hands.

"Not my penis! No! I command you to relent!"

The troll didn't listen and mangled the member, then stuffed it in his mouth and began chewing it. With each chomp Satan convulsed as though the penis was still attached and able to feel pain. Astaroth was dancing in circles and cackling and throwing his head back, jerking around in a random way as the troll let out a sound like a boulder tossed into a deep canyon- perhaps laughter of sorts. Watching what was happening, Germaine laughed slightly and Satan shot him a dirty look through tears of pain and embarrassment.

A troop of demons soon came and began dragging the crying Satan back towards the hills, all the while their charge yelling insults and threatening revenge beyond comprehension. Gran stepped out from the embankment and, to the astonishment of all onlookers, began petting the troll and gave him a cake of sorts, which the beast smashed into its face, smearing the dough and frosting across itself until it looked like a deformed Santa Claus. "Don't worry about this one" she said "he's as gentle as a lamb." It burped and groaned and sat down and made noises at her, maybe a form of primitive conversation. She responded in kind, probably trying to learn troll-speak.

"I'm very sorry about that" Astaroth said in a hoarse voice, still standing in the street. "I told him it was a stupid idea but he always tests his friends, he's always causing trouble, he's like a big baby and cries when he watches chick flicks. You have no idea what I go through."

"So you're his gay friend?"

Astaroth was taken aback and grimmaced. "I'm more like his dad than a friend, I have to constantly repair the damage he does when he goes crazy. He beats his soldiers and I have to make sure they get healed. He rapes people at Christmas parties. He injures himself then whines like a bitch." He poked at his shirt and it turned into a sort of tattered toga, shimmering as it transmogrified at the touch of a demon. "So yes, sorry about that. I'll make sure to send some troops to help you build your barriers and maybe a field for your food or something, would that suffice?"

"Yes but, why would Satan celebrate Christmas?"

"Oh, he just wants presents."

Astaroth took flight then and bid them farewell, promising again to send aid. Before leaving he also took a chunk of Satan's penis which had fallen from the mouth of the troll when it had been eating. He indicated that it could be used in a manner like that of a voodoo doll, rendering Satan mostly impotent if he ever wanted to come cause trouble again. This spiritual icon was quickly stored in a little box on the altar of the church.

SICKNESS IN HELL

XIII: SATAN'S KINDNESS

The old woman whom Germaine had spoken to and who had promised to aid them all against Satan didn't show up until the subsequent day. With the entire area littered with corpses, and hordes of flies swarming them all, it would have been a miserable sight for her to behold, but the corpses were quickly dotted with mushrooms and Germaine determined that if they laid them all out sliced in half front to back they could reasonably make a mushroom farm. The sun didn't seem to harm the fungus, and Dawn volunteered to chop the bodies apart with a chainsaw.

Muttering about other business, the necromantic hag told Germaine that soon they could expect an influx of newcomers because she had been sheltering them in her basement and feeding them dead possums, excusing her absence and bemoaning her busy schedule. She didn't seem too busy to him, as she stood there scratching her breasts crudely, the bottom of her labia swinging back and forth under her skirt, which was a few inches too short due to fraying and tearing.

"I have some goodies for you all." She waved at the treeline and out came lumbering several strange creatures.

The first was a tree, but it wasn't a plant, it was made entirely of meat, or seemed to be so- with branches and twigs of muscle, little bony leaves without any photosynthetic material at all, roots like giant knots of flesh lumbering forth like the limbs of a crab spider, curling into the dirt and plowing it loose as it stepped forth, settling in across from the embankment and planting itself there, giving a little shake as it settled in.

There were also a pair of what appeared to be Irish Wolfhounds, only bigger, much bigger, each the size of a moose, each one laden on either side with burlap sacks of some sort filled, he imagined, with food or something.

The tree swung out a limb and released what appeared to be seeds. These little, walnut-sized nubs of muscle tissue quickly disappeared into the plowed dirt behind the tree, and sprouted- transforming into miniature meat-trees, sitting there oozing as they leeched the soil.

"The sacks have food, the tree is for protection, it will smash anything to bits with its limbs. I have three of them at my home but, I think I'd rather come live here and bring the rest of my little friends."

Peter was terrified of the labia-woman and shook his head slightly as Germaine gazed across to him, sitting there on his fused legs slightly off to the side and behind the woman; Dawn was a bit less hesitant but failed to affirm the idea.

"Are you sure? Look at this mess."

He pointed at the church. Several chunks of its outer wall were gone and the entire yard was a smear of blood with random piles of demon junk cluttering it up. Spindly bro had literally begun cutting the armor apart and bolting it back together into what he hoped would be his own plate armor suit. His sister was sweeping the dirt with a rake and trying to move the blood-soaked, contaminated mess away to the sides before the rain they could already smell in the distance, lest the entire area go entirely to pot.

"Don't worry your pretty little heads about me, I'm bringing you food aren't I? I'm a witch, aren't I?"

None of them wanted to piss off someone who could apparently animate lifeless matter at a whim so they agreed in brief discussion to admit her. She cackled with delight.

"You have made a good choice, I will now help you a little more."

She waved her hand and stuck the other into her shirt to titillate her titties- by her power a wall of rock was wrenched loose from the dirt and floated lazily up to the gaping holes in their fortress, sliding into place with such ease that it would have been difficult to slip a sheet of paper between the stones there, as they morphed in shape, malleable under her spell, and squeezed together like putty. Another wave of her hand piled all of the debris in the yard into the barricades, save for a few interesting things that she said she wanted for herself- a demon head, a couple of knives, and so forth.

The repairs were thus complete, at least externally, she ran off into the woods cackling to retrieve her "friends" and left Peter, primarily, to attempt to piece together some of the shattered wooden panels and flooring inside the tower and at other parts of the church which had been hit by Pillwaff's boulders. He had a good time of it, since he had taken a significant number of urns of demon liquor from the pile of corpses outside, and was heavily inebriated- this didn't help his aim with the hammer but he was too drunk to care when he mashed his thumb with such force that it split like an overcooked hot dog, bending down to suck his own churning, purple fluids out of the mutilated digit.

Astaroth arrived not too long after, reporting that Satan felt sorry for what he had done and hoped that it didn't mean they didn't love him anymore. He flourished a solid gold record in Germaine's face and said it was a gift right from the devil himself along with all the other goods he had for them- several trolls hauling iron-coated wooden sections for an outer wall, more hauling wagons stacked with bricks for a nice garden, even more filtering up the road by twos, carrying beams, roofing material, iron poles, weapons, food, crates and crates of what Astaroth told them were bottles of mushroom nectar which could be used to heal wounds. After a few minutes so many trolls and attendant demonic imps and hobgoblins were crowding the yard that the noise became unbearable, between the frequent chattering of the latter and the grunting and roars of the former- Germaine took Astaroth aside indoors, where the trolls at least weren't able to follow.

"So Satan isn't going to do this crap again?"

"I doubt it, he'll probably leave you gifts for a while

like a scolded cat to make up for the loss of your friend. Oh yes, about your friend by the way, the one rotting on the altar."

He took Germaine along for a walk through the hall into the main room, where Adam was still laying on the slab of god, growing more and more bloated and purple by the moment.

"There is a way to revive him, but you should expect some... side effects."

Germaine nodded but was partially distracted by Astaroth fiddling around in his pocket. He withdrew a little vial no more than two inches long, and lined near the neck of the little thing with tiny projections like glass spines, decorative and shiny, the vial itself filled with a dimly glowing red substance of sorts.

"This is the elixir, the universal medicine, it is the red lion." He waved it slowly back and forth and grinned. "Your friend can be revived because there is now a direct link between Hell and your world- your friend, at the moment, is physically embodied in the former. Kill him in Hell and give the corpse this drink and it will be done. As I said, a warning about side effects, he won't be the same as before, because the rot and decay will not fully be removed."

"So he'll be a zombie?"

Astaroth shook his head, "No, that's not what I'm

SICKNESS IN HELL

saying, he'll be just fine, but, well, just watch if you want
me to do this."

He nodded, thinking to himself that maybe Adam
would end up a mindless mutant like some of the others
he'd tangled with since his brain had surely, by now, mostly
rotted into a mass of gelatin. Astaroth called for his
messenger and told him to depart immediately and hold
netherworld-bound Adam's physical body and to kill the
same at exactly ten o'clock, making sure to tell the
legalistic imp "that means morning, not afternoon."

Five minutes passed and it was time. Astaroth gazed
at a stopwatch he had in one hand and, as the arm passed
over the twelve, he pulled down Adam's lower jaw and
emptied the mix into his throat. The compound steamed
and sizzled, and crackled as it pooled up there then got
sucked inside as the corpse, formerly immobile, inhaled
like a reverse death rattle, and then spewed it all back out.

He sat bolt upright on the slab, and gave a long and
frantic yell, flailing around and knocking Germaine on his
ass, his bloated, rotting body there looking with sunken
eyes at nothing and yet at everything in the room in quick
succession. After a moment of this apparent terror, he
stopped, blinked, grabbed the slab below him with great
vigor, looked down, and contemplated his existence for a
moment, then gasped.

He tried to speak but apparently a good deal of
rotting tissue had liquefied and filled his lungs. He quickly
gave a little inhalation then forced the air out, along with a

massive stringer of greenish corpse blood and phlegm, the mass, sticky and horrible, clinging to his chest as he tried and failed to dislodge the sticky lung-boogers.

He managed, through additional fluid, to gobble out a simple sentence; "I was dead, wasn't I?" He gasped again, then said "I'm all fucked up."

He grabbed his chest and tugged at it, peeling off the flesh entirely there, exposing the rancid organs within, drippy and clinging to his fat cells, which had partially denatured like a heated protein and begun to resemble a kitchen sponge covered in toothpaste more than the rubbery little nodules they had prior. He shoved the cavity closed again and shook his head "At least I'm not dead anymore."

With hundreds of demons working in tandem and the raw strength of their attendant trolls, work was swift. Astaroth and Dawn largely directed the construction itself, but it was Adam, leaning against a pile of bricks and trying not to decompose, who oversaw the construction of what he hoped would become a sort of large enclosed garden space.

Two trolls, larger than the rest by a few feet in height and covered from head to toe in leather panels, shoved a drill into the earth in the center of the yard, around which lines of goblin-esque demons were plowing out the turf and laying down foot-thick blocks of organic debris- a mulch, Astaroth declared- made from rotted mushrooms and bone chips, as fertile ground for their fungal feeding frenzy. The yard being about an acre and a half in total size, the work would have taken months without demonic aid- Astaroth advised Adam that his body would begin to recover and offered him a massive slab of corned beef. Adam shook his head, still feeling sick and weak.

"I strongly suggest you eat this."

A few nibbles later he was already beginning to recover. Surprised, he continued, gulping down ravenous mouthfuls of the stuff and pouring a bit of demon liquor down despite himself.

"Remember, you kind folk don't need pills or surgeries, you have a mutual symbiosis with the fungus lodged in every one of your organs and tissues, and you just need to feed it. It can reanimate dead tissue, it can refresh old matter."

Adam continued to stuff the meat into his maw, and was additionally elated when his deformed feet began to return to a slightly more normal semblance of humanity. "Oh yes I spiked the meat with elixir, if you ever get too horribly mutated or feel like the sickness is driving you mad, take a sip of that stuff and it will stave off both deformity and lunacy. This will be important." He turned to Germaine and beckoned him over. "I was explaining" he said as Germaine approached, "to your friend, the importance of the elixir, behold his feet." He pointed and Germaine nodded lightly in approval at his friend's remarkable transformation. "I will teach you in time how to make more of the elixir- it isn't too easy but once you get the hang of it, it will serve you well, and you don't need an awful lot of it- a sip or two for even the worst effects of mushroom sickness, mental or physical."

"It's a sickness? I thought Satan said it was a blessing?"

"Oh it is. Let me explain." He cleared his throat and inhaled and Germaine immediately knew he was going to get a lecture. "A normal human so-called will live for seventy, eighty, maybe ninety years or so- if they make it to a hundred they consider themselves lucky, but from the moment they're born their bodies begin to slacken on the bone, grow older, and lose their malleability- it is change that revives and allows one to thrive- but the only change happening in a human, normally, is that their cells and organs begin to lose their ability to change- their malleability- they change into a lack of change."

This made surprisingly more sense than Germaine had anticipated, and Adam wasn't about to interrupt since he had three or four pounds of flesh in his hands and nothing but his mouth to cram it into. "You on the other hand are symbiotes with fungus. Fungus is wonderful; there are mushrooms that live only by absorbing radiation, there are mushrooms that will grow in a stratum so acidic that it would burn a hole in your hand, there are fungus species whose only purpose is to decompose the dead- and when they do so they bring life to inanimate material, they are the recyclers. Now, normally, before, this recycling only takes place when one being dies and the mushrooms recycle its flesh- they decay and the mushrooms transmogrify the dead flesh of, say, a person or a tree, into a living hyphae and thence into a mushroom cap, or some mold, or something like that. But you are not the same, you recycle your own dead tissues and continuously renew them. This process isn't all that intensive, you just have to eat as you did before, perhaps you will be a little more hungry, and if the symbiotic fungus is out of balance and begins to creep into your brain and take over, or you feed too much and start growing extra limbs you dislike, you take some elixir and it will destroy some of the symbiote."

"So it's the only medicine we will need?"

"Kind of, food is also your medicine when wounded, and you won't be getting ill any time soon since the fungus inside you is immune to any human disease. A disease of fungus will be destroyed by your human immune system. A disease of human tissue will be destroyed by the fungus which will consume it. It is a perfect duality. I must warn you above all else though to never take more than a sip or two of elixir- more than that could destroy the symbiosis inside you and turn you back into a human, only one who is deformed and physically unable to maintain their significantly more metabolically active form- and the only solution would be to reintroduce the species into your flesh by consuming mushrooms that now are no longer guaranteed not to immediately go to your brain and kill you off."

His lecture over, the demon smiled warmly, turned a half-step and went back to watching the construction. Adam was burping and couldn't respond. Germaine didn't feel compelled to, since this particular being seemed a bit more trustworthy and less sketchy perhaps than his master.

By the end of the afternoon, as the sun began to wane, the church itself was completely repaired, along with the second wall they had begun constructing only of debris- now it was an imposing line of wooden planks sheeted on the outside with iron panels, bolted to a steel frame on the inside which went into the ground some three feet, and stood about seven feet tall. Five small towers along it allowed those inside to peer beyond, and these rose an additional ten feet into the air and were a bit more solidly built.

The interior wall had also been scrapped- with this taller outer barrier it was no longer needed and merely took up room. Astaroth arranged a rough plan of what would eventually be a little village of sorts- the church, the mushroom yard, several small homes, a sort of multipurpose building he indicated would perhaps serve best as barricades or a motel, and an underground area connecting all of these together with an antechamber below for storage and perhaps defense.

"You will have the ability to requisition anything outside of the wall too, remember, but it would behoove you to settle in here first."

He indicated the delineation of the mushroom garden was large enough to feed them all and, in time, to process elixir. That wasn't of course their only food source, just one they all happened to enjoy, protected by their wall.

SICKNESS IN HELL

The meat tree outside shook and began to wave its nodule-coated meat branches around flexing its tree muscles and making hideous squelching noises at them all. Astaroth was as surprised as the rest of them when it cartwheeled on its outstretched roots and branches over the outer wall and settled into the rich dirt of the yard. With a little twist it embedded itself there and sucked out some nutrients, then let loose a blast of little brown lumps that looked like deer shit.

Holding one of the golfball-sized lumps up to the dying sunlight, Germaine tossed it aside in fear as it began to shudder and make crackling noises. What emerged from this little shell of sorts was a gadfly of some sort- a little insectoid of meat that twisted around and then took off, along with its compatriots emerging from dozens of other turd-eggs; the selfsame little creatures flew straight into the bell tower and almost immediately began to nest there.

"Life is a wonderful thing isn't it?" Astaroth chuckled and rubbed his hands together in a gleeful manner, hunching over as he did, choking back his own spittle. "I won't return for some time but I will leave some of the demons here to continue the other work you require to live here in a semblance of comfort. We have some experiments we're creating right now that I think you will find most interesting."

The arch-demon himself mounted the wall, shoved his naked ass against it leaving a brown streak, and flew off to the hills as the company settled in for the night.

XIV: THE NEXT STRUGGLE

Indeed the Necromantic old woman had been correct; around the time that the outer barrier was complete, Adam, still tending the shortwave broadcast he had rigged in the church to begin with, began to work; the first indication was a slightly garbled reply as he switched through various wavelengths and rambled about Satan- but soon several dozen newcomers had filed into the little village as refugees.

They were all decrepit, they were all mutated- one of them, a woman named Sally, had grown so vestigial that her entire body was curled into a circle, her chin roughly fused to her lower back such that her mouth was inches from her anus, and in this condition she was forced to roll herself around using her arms, like a sort of strange human wheel, or a hoopsnake, or a tire come to life under some sort of malevolent hex. Remembering Astaroth's wisdom, Germaine dispensed a few drops of elixir to this unfortunate being, and with enormous speed, her flesh there came loose and the fusion was broken; soon she was able to stand upright, more or less, although she remained hunched over in a hideous way and though she begged for another dose, the prohibition of the same was echoed. Forsaking reason, she managed to snatch the vial and drained it, eyes wide with expectation, and Germaine and his sister exchanged knowing, slightly saddened glances at one another as she convulsed and fell over, her vestigiality melting away visibly.

SICKNESS IN HELL

Left now mortal again, at first she was elated, until she began gagging on the spore-rich air, choking and vomiting. Expecting her to pass out and wake up with her mind burned out and no cognition beyond hunger left, Dawn put her out of her misery with a quick smack to the back of the head with a hammer and tossed her dead body in the mushroom pit to decompose, but not before chewing her ears off and swallowing them as a lunchtime dessert.

More cooperation was obtained from the others who had come; most of them were children- a few weren't even past the toddler stage, and these tyrannical toddlers were an order of magnitude more prone to climbing, consuming, and slapping everything in their path than toddlers were to begin with. One of them clambered up the side of the church, aided by an extra pair of arms, both sets of the same spindly and hairy like those of a spider. It perched atop the bell tower and jumped right off, shrieking with glee as it smashed into the side of the meat tree and began gnawing it. The tree, disliking such antics, swatted the attacker off to the side, where it rolled, stopped, cried for a moment, and quickly lost interest, hurrying off to chase after a few squirrels which had begun nesting in a pile of trash. The kid managed to scare them up the side of the tree, and it pounded one of the itchy, scurrying little thing in the neck and flailed its muscular limbs insanely at the corpse as it bounced from branch to branch on its way down to be eaten by the children.

Indeed only three of the roughly twenty five new arrivals were fully mature- the rest were toddlers or children which had apparently been in their early teens at most before departing.

"So, are you all neighbors or something?" Germaine wondered how so many of them had come to travel together.

The oldest, a man with a beard so mutated that it was literally fused to his chest, spoke up, waving his hands around in great happiness at having found some semblance of civilization. "No, these kids were just wandering around, we-" he gestured at himself and the other two adults- "were neighbors, and we heard your radio, and we weren't that far off, we're from Greenville, about a hundred miles South. Halfway here we were attacked by this horde."

"You were attacked so you let them come with you?"

"No, we were attacked, then some cows wandered by, they were starving and dying, and we all ended up devouring them, I think we're messed up because that raw, bloody meat tasted better than any steak I ever had. We set back out and the kids just sort of followed us."

"I'm not a kid." The oldest, who had been wearing some sort of denim rocker outfit before being horribly disfigured, half his face burned off, probably in some sort of accident, spoke now. "Hey can I have one of those guns?"

Dawn was already reaching for one and Germaine figured that laws related to bearing automatic weapons were as vestigial as the third boob Dawn was slowly growing on her chest by rubbing it with mushrooms and poking herself repeatedly with a needle. The boy took it and jogged off to go get some cans and bottles to practice his aim.

"Honestly" Germaine said, "we just got finished with preparing this whole place, you may not believe me but we had help from a bunch of demons. I went to Hell a few days ago, and I barely believe it myself."

The only younger adult in the group indicated that they had already seen some of the beings he referred to- they described them and Germaine decided that Astaroth must have passed them on the way back, and had been riding a troll at the time. "Well that's good, then I don't sound like a madman I suppose."

Everyone was quickly settled in- all the children ended up in the barracks; the three adults who had come chose to requisition a home outside of the innermost barrier and quickly piled some wood and rocks around it, taking a couple of rifles and knives and some food. The bearded guy wanted to scout around the entire town since he hadn't seen it before, and they declared that they would "brutalize" any attackers dwelling in the area. This was actually a welcome idea; after all, with all that had been going on they hadn't been able to go house to house to destroy any of the more mindless sort of mutants that happened to still be alive there.

The quick population increase, though, came

attendant with its own problems.

The first problem was food; the children were eating at a massive rate because their metabolism had to support both their normal growth and healing all of their toddler boo-boos; since they were frequently attacking one another and injuring themselves by falling off of the barrack roof and out the windows, this was quite a task; they went through a whole crate of goods just in the first day.

The second problem was noise and stress; the same children were a lot louder than "normal" children- Gran helpfully solved this problem by nominating herself as school teacher and babysitter; this was a huge relief since Adam had gotten tired of them nibbling his feet every time he went in to bring them a pile of slop to gargle on.

The third problem was arguments; Germaine insisted that there should be no rule of law at all and that their community should simply do what needs to be done. Adam wanted to form a sort of quasi-republic, and Dawn rubbed her hands together and declared that she wanted to establish a dictatorship and rule the world. She was being sarcastic but the debate devolved into a shit fest of everyone offering reasons why one or the other form of governance was superior to all others. Thankfully for Germaine, in the end it all came down to whether anyone was willing to splatter someone else on the ground with a machete for not obeying an order, and there was nobody to really give orders- a sort of libertarian voluntaryism took root without even being willfully implemented, since everyone was at an impasse.

It was generally decided that there would have to be some specialization of labor. Adam was overjoyed at the turn of conversation and said that he had always been of the opinion that it should exist alongside generalization; everyone should be trained in, and able and permitted to do, the same basic things, but everyone should also find something else that interests them and that they're tolerably good at to specialize in. This seemed logical; Adam had his radio and his apparent knowledge of engineering, Dawn was a pure warrior of sorts, Germaine tended towards planning and strategy.

Peter was happy too- he wanted to take his son out on ventures into the county at large to scavenge goods and probably hatchet a few enemies if they were ever encountered, but his daughter, who he also included in this desire, was more interested in tending the crops, and said she wanted to wall off an area adjacent to the little village and make her own garden.

Though she spoke with a wheeze due to facial scarring, the girl managed to relate her abilities. "If I can find the right equipment I should be able to make all sorts of crops and trees and things, I can use the fungus as an intermediary, and just use the same methods anyone would find in a high school lab to introduce luciferase into an E Coli bacterium."

"You won't even need to do that dear." The necromantic old woman was standing behind her and chimed in, grinning as she clasped her hands together briefly, opening them to reveal a sort of glowing, purple spider hunched down in her palms there. "We can always use magic too, I will teach you."

This relatively quicker method was accepted and the old woman led charred sis off into the hinterland to gather seeds and mutate them.

Thus it seemed like the new problems they were facing were more or less solved; the inside offices of the church were partitioned and, in expectation of perhaps new arrivals at any time, they left four of the interior rooms empty. The only new problem faced was the smell; all of these mutants gathered in one place had led to a severe case of people pissing and shitting and oozing pus in the dirt, and it was piling up notably, especially in the little alley formed between the barracks and the back of the church itself.

"Adam is there any way we can get the plumbing to work again? I think the explosion at the plant disrupted the pipes or something."

"No, the plumbing is fine, I had turned the water valves off myself. I'll turn them back on, but the church only has two bathrooms."

"Can we build more?"

"A tall order since we don't have any piping, and we don't have a plumber around. I dabbled with electrical work and architecture but I don't know shit about toilets."

"I do!" A voice spoke up in the general hubbub of passers-by. The voice came from a kid no more than ten years old. "There used to be videos on the internet where people would talk about toilet models and how they worked and all sorts of stuff, and they'd test the flushing pressure and everything. I watched them all the time, I can help you!" His forehead had become so deformed that his eyes were little more than slits below its canyon-esque surface, each massive ridge standing out with a line of cartilage, wubbering back and forth like the belly of a diseased and obese animal.

The idea of a child being their plumber was not to Germaine's liking, but Dawn thought this was adorable and walked him off to the side to discuss the relative virtues of different models, and she had some aesthetic ideas of her own. Adam shrugged and muttered about how reality wasn't real anymore and "kids these days," but Germaine was slightly angry at not having the chance to get a bit more explanation before committing to having a ten year old crawling around fixing the plumbing.

"Dawn... sis... hey!" He poked at her and interrupted an extremely interesting conversation about vintage toiletries.

"What, oh interrupt-y one?"

"Are we sure this is a good idea?" He turned to the kid "What's your name by the way, and what if you end up like speared by a toilet pipe or something?"

"Zak, and no, don't worry, I used to fiddle around all the time with my uncle's plumbing, he would get drunk and fall asleep and I'd spend hours doing that- he had five old toilets that I set up."

Dawn shot him a nasty look, the "You'll crush his dreams and by god if you do and I don't get my fancy toilet I'll wring your neck and stab out your eyes" look- he sighed and wandered off to go sit next to Adam, who had now taken a liking to demon rum, and stole the jar from him to take a good draft of the stuff. This batch was, at least, better than before, and didn't taste like someone dropped a dollop of habenero salsa in a bottle of vodka and sprinkled nutmeg in it.

Everything was fairly set up within only a few weeks. Charred sis had constructed her garden, but wouldn't let anyone see it until it was "absolutely complete." Zak had successfully set up a row of three outhouses in the shitting alley, and their food supply had been somewhat improved by additional mushroom beds dug out by beard man and his neighborhood clan- every time they macerated a mindless mutant they tossed the chopped up body in their own shroom pit, and Peter and his spindly spawn had brought back a good month's worth of food in just two days when they discovered one resident's home who had been a survivalist. His dead body, laying in his garage, showed how useless his efforts were, but he had a massive supply of canned goods and that was worth more than a nut anyways.

CHAPTER XV: HEMMORHOID HENRY

It didn't take their new friend Zak long to rig up additional plumbing within the church in addition to the outhouses outside- this was a welcome relief, since now the area smelled mostly of mushrooms and blood, which was arguably more palatable than human waste- indeed everyone there remarked on the oddity of the same fermenting fungus having a rather pleasant aroma. Adam managed to help out primarily with the wooden shacks themselves which were little more than three-walled little rectangular structures like over-sized refrigerators with screen doors on the fronts paneled with plywood for privacy, the same doors having been ripped off of surrounding homes for this use.

It didn't take long for Charred sis to complete her garden finally as well. She and the necromancer (for that is what she referred to herself as, and the term stuck in the minds of everyone else) had developed quite a little area off to the side and pretty soon a little gate was plopped into the wall around it- the two of them looked gleeful as they announced the grand opening of a smorgasbord there, which they promised was tastier than just mushrooms alone. Charred sis was probably smiling but her mutilated face didn't have the mobility necessary to show it on the surface.

What was inside was like a warped little wonderland of strange flora and fauna- they had gone well beyond just developing plants for eating, in their wild experimentation, and the little area, which was perhaps fifty feet in diameter and roughly ovular, held a series of eight irregularly shaped garden beds, each of which had a different species within it- mutated flies buzzed around overhead, and strange amphibious creatures lazed around in the centerpiece around which all other beds revolved- a sort of little stagnating puddle at most two feet in depth with a little pump attached which acted like a fountain, dripping down the side of a huge chunk of concrete roughly shaped into a giant vulva.

A phosphorescence permeated the entire extent of the little garden, and there were a couple of shrubby trees there that were wriggling around and which had long, spindly branches that appeared to possess a cognitive ability- for they wrenched themselves slowly side to side, with a bit of creaking, apparently undulating around like sea anemones- the old woman, still waving her hand around and releasing little puffs of phosphorescent vapor which settled into the soil and caused it to glow- explained that they were carnivorous and would catch insects for sustenance, not just feed from the soil.

Behind the first of these strange shrubs was a bed full of plants which looked absolutely deadly- they were jagged, shiny, almost like little spikes of obsidian sticking out of the ground. Charred sis held up her hands, encouraging everyone to observe, and then lowered a severed arm into the bed. With a sound like that of a sprung bear trap, several of these spikes enclosed themselves around the arm, slicing it into chunks, which fell into the soil and almost immediately began decomposing into a

SICKNESS IN HELL

foaming mass of off-white fungus.

"A little trash disposal bed I suppose" she quipped.

Other strange little plants like multicolored clumps of moss, which they claimed were edible and impossible to kill, were growing irregularly, scattered around in each bed, even climbing up the inner wall of the garden enclosure- but it was the rear bed which caught Germaine's eye.

"What's that?" He pointed to a large mound in the earth, where it looked like something had recently been buried.

"Our newest floral acquisition. I think you will find this one extra horrid!" The necromancer cackled and chomped on a finger bone, dislodging one of her rotting teeth, sucking at the gum stump and swallowing the pus slowly oozing out of the wound. "It took quite an effort to make this one."

They led everyone to that same back bed, the toddlers of their big happy family wandering around and being wrangled away from the what Germaine had already mentally termed the "knife plants" in the disposal bed, and the old woman poked the mound with a long stick which she had leaning against a shrub right next to it. The mound began to shake and push upwards, and the dirt began crumbling away from whatever was underneath.

What was actually underneath was a man- or what apparently had been a man at some time in the past- his flesh was a sickly gray color, his nose was missing, and his fingers were crudely sewn together and the forearms sewn to his sides, where he tugged as he struggled up out of the soil, stretching the knitting and pulling his loose skin on both ends.

"This is Henry!" The old woman looked positively glowing, like someone whose cancer was just declared in remission, or a cat which just bit the head off a sparrow and had gorged on its corpse. Henry didn't look as pleased as the old woman did.

The man was covered in sores, or what at first anyways appeared to be sores. There, ensconced between a shrub and a patch of admittedly attractive little clumps of colorful moss, was this sad being rooted to the ground by his feet, which had twisted and elongated into the dirt, wrinkled and purple and hideous. The sores on his body turned out to be more than just wounds though, for as the crowd looked on, they opened up all at the same time and little drizzly plops of shit came sloughing out as he winced and groaned. The poop shots dropped into the bed around him and almost instantly began to fizzle with fungal malignancy, piling up as he apparently converted common dirt into waste.

"Isn't he lovely? I think I want more of these trees." The necromantic woman was drooling a bit and looking at Henry like she wanted to fornicate with his shit piles, but Germaine thought this might be a little over the top, perhaps a little bit unethical for his taste.

SICKNESS IN HELL

"Now, was this man a complete maniac, like the zombie people that we keep seeing, or was he able to talk and stuff?"

"I can talk, you savage little fuck."

The tree was talking to him, squinting his half blind eyes, coated in a layer of dirt, his sallow face shining under the sun, his skin having been stripped of its hairs all around until he resembled a corpse more than a living, breathing being. "Tell this crazy whore to kill me and put me out of my misery. Now!"

He was taken aback. So, clearly, were most of the others there; except for the old woman and Charred Sis; one of the toddlers was sniffing and doing the typical pre-crying ritual of a child which had been bothered by something they found a bit sad.

"Oh come on we can't enslave people just to harvest their shit, that's nuts. Go find a zombie and do that stuff to them instead."

The necromancer fiddled nervously with her finger bone. "No! My tree, and you can't do anything anyways, he's enchanted, and *you* don't practice magics like I do. You can go to Hell."

Dawn gave him a look, as if to say "maybe we were right about her being too insane." He didn't really want a confrontation with someone who can apparently cause a boulder to fly through the air or who could summon a legion of golems to her side, but watching the sad tree man covered in anuses from top to bottom seemed like his idea of an un-fun afternoon.

Thankfully for Germaine a little help was peering through a crack in the boards behind the woman. They all stopped their banter when they heard a little high pitched chuckle there, and in a moment, Satan's face appeared above the fence. His chuckle elevated in tone until it was nothing shy of a piercing laughter with the highest possible degree of merriment.

"Oh woman you have to learn to play nice with others." He vaulted over the fence, wearing nothing at all, his schlong dangling between his legs with a double set of testicles filling out his scrotum to the size of a football. He lifted one leg and let out a massive fart that shriveled the bush behind him into a pile of sediment and waved a hand, immediately setting Henry free, withdrawing his deformed feet from the soil and restoring them to their former usage.

"I'm not doing anything about your body-anuses though, they're too funny, and I think in time you will find them useful. As for you" he turned towards the necromancer "will you kindly please stop that?"

She looked repentant, muttered, and pretended to ignore the proceedings, wandering to the side to fiddle around with a bed of enormous plants like prolapsing cabbages. "I'm sorry about that; one time she gave poor Astaroth a pair of dicks that wouldn't stop hitting each other like a pair of snakes competing over a dead rat."

SICKNESS IN HELL

Peter and Adam had weapons in hand and were ready to attack Satan, not fully realizing that he was an ally that only occasionally caused problems for his own amusement, and Germaine had to push their hands away from their holsters. Henry scrambled out of the dirt mound and cursed the old woman, grabbing up a shovel and preparing to attack her. Satan stopped him and grabbed the shovel with his gnarly hands.

"Not a great idea."

The frustrated tree man pooped out a little bit of creamy diarrhea from his various orifices in response, and caused the Devil to bite his lip trying not to laugh at him, causing perhaps more frustration. Poop was pooling up at his feet.

"I expect repayment for this."

"Are you staying here? We have a strict 'don't fuck others over' policy." Dawn looked him up and down like a person evaluating the sad state of a dog which had just gotten into a tangle with a porcupine and whose face now looked like a pin cushion. "We weren't aware that you were being tormented."

"I'll forgive all of you, but I don't want her anywhere near me" he gestured at the necromancer, still bent over her cabbages and muttering with malevolence, hexing small insects with delight and torturing them with telekinetic force. "I was coming here anyways to live, I heard your radio thing, and when I got near the wall I fainted. When I came to, I was buried in dirt and this old woman was standing there naked and saying terrible things to me about wanting to chew my penis off for a thousand years."

The necromancer reacted by laughing heartily, as though her statements to him, in all their evil, were the funniest thing she ever heard. "Oh you crazy whore, I should put this shovel through your neck and hoist you up on a tree and beat your body until all your guts slop out."

This only made the woman horny, or so it seemed, because her flappy vulva suddenly leaked with cottage cheese curds and she tugged them open and thrust a stick inside her vagina, going glazed and not responding at all. Henry continued to stare her in the eyes, shovel ready to smash her skull if she got too close.

"Well I guess I'm glad you're staying here. You two shouldn't interact though." Germaine shook his hand after offering it for an awkward moment, the man reaching out to shake Germaine's but missing twice because he refused to take his eyes off the old woman, who was still crudely fumbling with herself and watching him with great lust.

"I heard you even had plumbing here. I haven't taken a normal shit for obvious reasons in two days."

Charred Sis seemed a lot more sorry about the event than the necromancer did- apparently Henry didn't realize she had been in on everything going on in the garden, and nobody was inclined to start more trouble by telling him

SICKNESS IN HELL

about the goings-on there.

Literally everyone was glad he didn't just flee off into the hinterlands as well. At regular intervals, he released trickling globules of waste from one or more of his bodily anuses, and each time the fermenting anal nectar dripped down onto the ground, this infected crap grew a little patch of mushrooms, which almost immediately absorbed the actual turds, converting it almost entirely within seconds. These tasty treats necessitated that he wander around mostly naked.

Back in the main yard, Satan spoke up. "Since you're technically growing food just by existing, I don't see any reason why you should be expected to do anything else unless you have a desire for it." He glanced at Germaine knowingly and winked, his cock throbbing a little as he licked his lips, apparently in a gay way as he grabbed the fence and vaulted back over it, chuckling as he departed.

It seemed like a generally decent idea; Henry's poop soon became as valued as gold, because whatever the necromancer had done to him, painful as it may have been, had infected him with so much fungus that his shit was growing hyphae before it even hit the ground. Adam said that he detected a slightly different flavor as well in these happy little shrooms- a bit like garlic perhaps, a nice little bite to the caps which were soon dotting everything indoors and out, greatly expanding their food production well beyond just their normal fungal gardening ventures.

CHAPTER XVI: NECROMANCY

The mutated folk now residing in this compact little village took to naming that settlement "New Hillcrest"- they saw no reason to take Peter's suggestion seriously and call it "Hell" or something like that. Dawn was afraid that to do so might bother Satan a bit, and then it would be likely he'd return to knock their walls down with his cock. For a couple of weeks, there was nothing but peace- it even seemed to become a bit of a lazy existence; no newcomers had arrived for some days and there was no construction to do, and between Hemmorhoid Henry's bowel drippings and their various farming endeavors, as well as scavenging goods from the slowly decaying remnant of the rest of the former town, they had several times more food than they needed. It turned out that food waste was no longer a thing- any time something spoiled it ended up growing edible mushrooms rather than mold, and even when mold did take hold, they ate that too, without apparent issue, their digestive systems being so massively riddled with mycelium to melt down poison and rot alike.

One thing was troubling Germaine slightly, however- the old necromancer woman had changed in attitude completely after being chastised for her gardening malevolence and had taken to shutting herself in a little shack she had erected on the other side thereof. Charred Sis hadn't reacted in such a manner; she didn't seem to care beyond tending the plants in what was generally a normal manner, but the sadistic old woman who had taught her the magickal craft now ignored everyone and occasionally prowled around the outer wall, muttering to herself and alternately cackling on her nearly toothless old maw, stopping only to take a piss on the wall, the acidity of the torrent of urine melting little holes in the wood. He'd asked her politely to put her burning vaginal effluence to use somewhere else and she pretended she was deaf when he did.

Peter and Dawn agreed when he related his worries to them, but Dawn laughed and told him he was probably just getting paranoid. Everyone had bad moods, she said.

"Bad moods don't usually last for weeks."

"Maybe she's getting demented, how old is she?"

He raised his eyebrows at the question to be sure, maybe she was a hold over from the Medieval era and just refused to die or something. He waved the question off "never mind, maybe she's going nuts, it just feels like something's up."

He glanced across the yard where Peter's son was helping Zak build a little ant colony (something he had apparently always wanted)- these ants were hardly ordinary for they had presumably become symbiotes to the same fungus as the rest of them; they were dusted with mycelium and their legs were massively long- they almost now looked more like a bunch of daddy longlegs' than the ants they once resembled. Now, though, everyone stopped doing what they had been, because they felt the Earth shake with massive force.

SICKNESS IN HELL

Wondering what the Hell was going on, Dawn was tossed to the side of the yard while Germaine staggered backwards and went straight through the window of the barracks, where their little porch overhand adjoined the side closest to the shitting alley. Peter, rooted to the ground with his rotund shape, simply tilted to the side and sat there with a stale beer, drunk enough to think the Earth was moving only because he was drunk.

The shaking, which had been vigorous enough to shatter several of the windows on the church, suddenly stopped, and each one of them staggered to their feet, before, in a moment, they all heard it- a distant yowling, like a crying cat only deeper, a throbbing sob that echoed over their outer wall. Curious as to these proceedings, Adam began to shuffle at maximum speed in the general direction along with Zak, who trailed him closely. Dawn was already arming herself, grabbing up an ax and whirling around, figuring better safe than sorry. Everyone else was too confused to react, but Germaine decided to follow his sister.

There, nailed to a tree beyond their wall roughly off to the side of the garden by thirty feet or so, was Satan himself, upside down, crucified there and howling with pain, the tip of his prehensile penis stretched out nearly flat on the trunk with a half dozen thumbtacks, the member wriggling against them, struggling to get free.

"You morons, get me down from here! It's the old woman, she's batshit!"

188

SICKNESS IN HELL

The old woman, which had been watching this spectacle from behind her shack, stepped out and guffawed at the pain of the Devil, stark naked there, her body gray and hideous, shriveled, her flesh sunken against her skeleton, her genitalia hanging in a grotesque manner, wubbering back and forth with the slightest movement. She was flanked by a pair of demons, which she had a hold of. They were trying to escape to get to their master but she was holding them fast with her enchanted fists. With a single movement, she gave a little twist and snapped their necks, dropping them to the soil, then took a whiz on them both, melting through their armor with a sizzle and a bit of smoke which wafted off of their degraded iron plates.

She stopped laughing and stared straight at the mutants there assembled.

"I will have my garden!"

"You crazy old woman." Henry was lumbering through now. "You're obsessed, go away." Instead of the shovel he had menaced her with weeks ago, he was holding a chainsaw and looked ready to chop her in half from crotch to neck. Dawn put out a hand to keep him from trying, since it wasn't at all clear that the woman was even capable of being killed.

Satan had managed to work his penis loose from the tacks holding it in place while the woman was distracted in conversation, and gave a quick nod to Germaine as he glanced sideways at the sight of this ropey phallus attempting to rip loose the nails holding him fast to the tree trunk, wrapping itself around them and tugging bit by bit. A nod that said "keep the bitch distracted."

"Why are you doing this?"

"I want my shit tree! I want my axolotl pond!" The woman began muttering, occasionally exclaiming in wild words all of the strange and apparently magickal things she wanted.

"What the fuck is an axolotl?"

The woman ignored him. She was kicking the melting demons at her feet and having another apparent moment of dementia. With the necromancer staring down at the ground Satan managed to get one foot loose, then wrapped his dick around a tree branch, reached up with this leverage, and ripped the other nail out, dismounting from the tree slowly so as not to let the woman know he was free. With another quick nod he tip-toed off into the bushes behind him, waving his hands sharply out in front of him, gesturing "I'll be back in a moment." To see Satan looking slightly alarmed was amusing but the magickal old broad before them was hardly funny.

"This is now my town. You must all leave."

She stepped back slowly and purposefully, waving her hand before her, flourishing it, and a sort of undulating purple fog emerged from it, settling down over the demons she had just killed. Their flesh began to pulsate, then liquefy, and soon was running out of their armor in torrents with a massive wafting blast of hot steam. Their bilge-filled guts leaked from the skeletons left behind and their degrading armor, and the skeletons then began to move; clawing their way through the guts and mud below, standing before them now, still armed, staring with lifeless, hollow eye sockets from which their brain fluid was leaking. This foulness trickled down from each socket, over the armor, and to the ground, like runny, melted cheese. The woman grabbed a bit of this and licked it off her spindly fingers, then jammed the rest onto her nipples, which were sagging down to her waist.

"Begone!" She stretched her hand forth again and her skeleton demons grabbed up their pikes and began attacking Adam, who was roughly in front. He smashed them both to the ground with little effort, but as soon as they were lying there still on the ground, they reanimated, stood up again, and continued. "That isn't all I can do."

She hurled a fireball in their general direction and they ducked to the side as it exploded in the bushes behind them, turning them to ashes, then she wheeled around and began spraying her purple fog everywhere on their little settlement. It worked its way into their mushroom yard and soon hundreds of skeletons were clawing their way through the mycelium to the surface, cracking it apart and digging themselves up and out like a regular army of the dead.

Realizing they were beyond their element, Germaine very quickly jogged back into the yard and yelled for everyone to grab what they could and clear out, alternately smashing his fist through the skeletons there and tossing the toddlers up over the wall, admonishing the others to do the same, grab whatever weapon was nearest, and flee into the brush.

Dawn and Adam joined in to try and debilitate this army while everyone else fled, while Peter literally grabbed Zak, put him on his back, and was the first to flee, the latter riding on the former like he was a walrus, flopping across the grass and flattening one skeleton in his way which was half formed and half out of the ground. He didn't even bother to requisition a hammer let alone the gun he had been storing in the church- it would have taken far too long.

Soon, with the children safely fleeing off after Peter, led by Peter's fire-scarred daughter and followed by Adam, who was bashing skeletons as they tried to follow, Germaine found himself paired only by Dawn, tossing weapons out of the yard with other necessities as the necromancer cackled from across the way, making no attempt to intervene and apparently enjoying the sight. They could hear a shriek of terror as the home outside the wall, where those adults who had most lately arrived, had been living, as a horde of skeletons smashed in through the windows there. He didn't have time to make sure they could escape, although their attackers seemed to go down fairly easily with no weapon at all. Hopefully they'd figure this out.

Gran came walking down the stairs in front of the church with a canesword, slashing and stabbing enemies out of her way, and didn't bother to run as she made her way past the wall and off into the brush, but their pet cat was not so lucky. These creatures were scaring it, and it was still up a tree trying to avoid them. He began walking through the crowd of milling skeletons to go get it down, but the necromancer fired a streak of bluish energy in front of him creating a sort of wall to keep him away.

"Take your things and go, the cat is mine!" She shrieked again with horrific delight and started whipping her chest around, her breasts, feet long, spinning around leaking cottage cheese drippings like a torrid windmill.

He didn't need to be told twice and, as he smashed through a last skeleton, he and his sister, carrying a number of weapons, hurried out of the walled enclosure. Behind them, their village was nothing but skeletons from one side to the other, the beings spilling out through the gate and wandering around the general area aimlessly. The meat tree tried to follow them in their retreat but was stunned by the woman as she cackled some more and bolted its roots to the earth.

"Where are we going to go now?" As they hurried after the others in the general direction of the center of town, Dawn looked like she was about to cry. This was displeasing, and pointless girl stuff, and Germaine told her as much.

"Doesn't matter, we'll figure it out."

In five minutes they caught up with the rest of them, Adam gleeful that they hadn't been taken captive and locked in a dungeon somewhere. He was also curious as to what the next move was- dispossessed of their fungal farm and most of their weapons, and laden with more children than adults, they were arguably vulnerable. What if, he asked, a bunch of zombie-mutants came after them out in the open where they had no fortifications?

"You should come with me of course."

Astaroth answered the question for Germaine, as he had been perched atop one of the row homes adjacent to the street they were on. "I saw what happened. Sorry that I didn't help out, this is going to require more than one archdemon to solve, sadly."

"Why did she go crazy? You seem to know everything so, you answer me."

"She's always been crazy. Everyone has always been crazy, but that's a tale for some other time." He was being smug, like he knew something nobody else in the group could know, that was an easily figured out secret that nobody could somehow grasp. "Just come to Hell with me for now, we've built a nice city already that none of you have ever seen, I think you will agree it's a sight to behold."

He led them now, across the same path that Germaine had previously walked on when the field gun had knocked him cold. It took an hour, but the rather long walk was infinitely worth it, for he took them to the top of the foothill there which stuck out into the little river valley East of Hillcrest and into the side of the mountain beyond- it had been massively fortified, spires and walls stretching up some two hundred feet, a regular wall of walls, crenelated with gargoyles and stone dicks, iron pikes covered in flags of a hideous color, each emblazoned with demonic seals and symbols. The main gate of this mountainside city, layered into five levels, was so large that ten men side by side could pass through it. There were troops of demons in full regalia marching through in platoons, and others, not in armor, scattered about chiseling and hacking through stone, others in large groups, rooms carved right into the rock, taking the raw stone and carving it more finely. The outer walls of each of the five levels were made of hewn stone layered as bricks, but the inner wall, behind the outer facade which was arranged in large, airy open pillars and archways, was nothing more than the rock of the mountain itself gutted and mined off, for other projects. Down below the mountain, on the selfsame foothill, a triple terrace was being build, apparently for an outer city of sorts.

"Down there there will be a wall and towers and many businesses, we will make a city upon this planet that will rival anything ever seen in the entire cosmos, and which is never likely to end. It will be an eternal city, the center of all the galaxy."

Satan himself was in the top level being tended to for his wounds, crying like a baby as antiseptic was applied, sucking his thumb and unresponsive when Astaroth announced that the "survivors had arrived." He then told Germaine that, sadly, those who had been in the home outside of the walls of New Hillcrest, the newly arrived adults, had all been captured, although they were not dead.

SICKNESS IN HELL

Once his treatment had ended and his penis was no longer covered in thumbtack marks, Satan was somewhat more receptive to conversation.

"She's a mean old woman" he said, fondling his wounds gently and holding a stuffed teddy bear in one arm, to comfort himself. "But we'll see who has better magick soon, I will wrap my penis around her neck and choke her to death and then impale her dead body above the gate of this city."

"If you're Satan can't you just wave your hand and rip out her soul or something?"

"It's a long story. I gave her some of my power a long time ago for being really good in bed. She told you, I presume, that we used to get off sometimes together. Anyways, back then I was kind of stoned, it was the disco and cocaine era. I made a few mistakes back then..." He trailed off and reached back to scratch his ass, then with a start, he stopped doing so as if it had been embarrassing. When Germaine beheld the Devil's ass he could see the faint remnants of a tattoo that had been removed; it appeared to be a picture of a clown fornicating with a bat. "But yes, it will take an actual army to get rid of her, I have to drain the power out of her and I can't do that without even more power being applied than I have. Thankfully she made a big mistake recently and it will be her undoing." He turned to Charred Sis. "She taught you her craft, did she not? My wonderful, dear lass." He chuckled and led her away with a shit eating grin.

CHAPTER XVII: THE FINAL BATTLE

The planning was the simple part, actually getting things organized was another story. The city had been designed as a formidable defensive structure and short of an atomic warhead its walls would be impermeable even to most modern weapons; that didn't mean that it was easy to march troops around it though; the outer system of roughly semi-circular paths were efficient but the confused mass of tunnels, caves, hallways, and antechambers built into the mountains themselves were a confusing and haphazard ordeal, modeled after Hell itself.

It took Satan a bit of effort to extract some of his troops from the lungshrimp pond too- he had carved out an enormous room at least a quarter mile long underneath the main chamber and the floor of the latter collapsed, sending several thousand of his own men into the water below- the pestilent parasites within quickly infested those unfortunate enough to fall, and it took Astaroth the better part of an hour- skipping to and fro from demon to demon- to administer a purgative. Each infected demon, in turn, let out an almighty squelching peal of dry heaves and inevitably got up some phlegm in which were mixed the dying bodies of dozens of these strange crustaceans, which wriggled their little legs around frantically and attempted to hop around up into the mouths of anyone nearby.

"Why did you create these?" Peter was taken aback, and he was more vulnerable than some, his face being low to the ground unable to stand normally. He whirled around and brought his abdomen down to crush any that tried to infect him.

"I thought it was funny, to make something so awful and pointless that anyone seeing it would ask 'why?' "

In due time a reasonable force had been assembled; Satan departed for a moment to go get suited up and returned with a pink school girl outfit and an enormous amount of makeup on. When queried he mumbled about French revolutionaries. There were ten columns of demons; each numbering five hundred in strength, and quite a number of ancillary forces riding trolls.

"Don't worry the air support is outside. Also, take these, all of you."

Satan beckoned to a small group of hobgoblins standing behind him and they brought out a number of strange shining devices that resembled the weapons Germaine had seen some of the troll-riders bearing before-the little crank-affixed guns which had puzzled him. These were handed out to all of the adults present, but Satan suggested that the children should remain behind.

"I want to come too!" Zak, being older than the other kids, didn't want to be identified with them.

"Not my decision my boy, ask your parents."

"They're dead."

SICKNESS IN HELL

He gave a look to Dawn and she nodded. The Devil sighed and patted the boy on the head, his skirt flapping around his legs in the wafting breeze of the airy hallways of his new metropolis. "Very well." He gestured again and a different weapon was brought forth- it was like a small handle with a projection in front of it, like the handle of a saber with no blade.

"Press the button." He pointed to the bottom of the device.

Zak did, and a strand of what at first appeared to be mercury dripped out of the handle down to the ground, for a moment, then the device let out a buzzing sound for just a moment and the fluid solidified, erected itself, and began to resemble a sort of rapier, only with a series of small spines scattered along its length; the blade, or whatever it was, was about two feet in length, a considerably grotesque looking apparatus.

"That thing will drain the blood right out of anything it touches so be wary." He turned to the others. "Those guns you have aren't guns, they are pin shooters. They will very quickly fire out their payload, which consists of extremely small strands of metal, which when they hit an object, tend to bend and shatter- at close range this will literally rip an enemy apart. They're useless for longer ranges but this war is going to look more like the Battle of Rorke's Drift than D Day. Everybody satisfied?"

Dawn was the only one who said anything, and what she said was more of a little, urging pouty noise.

SICKNESS IN HELL

"Oh yes I forgot, you're the firebug." He chuckled in a surprisingly warm manner, like an old widowed man whose child had just gotten a six figure position and sent him a block of cocaine and a sports car to seduce pickup artists with. "Here you are."

He produced from a small sack on his back, an even smaller sack, and handed it off to her. "Look inside."

Within were a few dozen small glowing balls, orange in color, about the size of grapes, or a little larger. "Careful not to drop those, they're basically fire grenades." This perked her up visibly.

"Time to go rape some ass!"

Germaine was about to ask if he meant 'kick' some ass but realized it was probably a stupid interjection. Satan had organized his troops in extremely rigorous fashion and had threatened to peel the skin off any of them that fled the battlefield once the fighting began, and boil anyone alive who fled before then. As to those present who weren't 'his' strictly speaking; Germaine and the rest, he mentioned prior that they could do whatever they wanted once the fighting began but that it was a horrifically bad idea to get too close to the necromancer- he, he said, would handle her himself.

The columns of demons began marching- somewhat slowly- from the main chamber to the hall beyond and out the gate, down around the little path through the lower level and through the final gate along the lowest outer wall some

200

distance below the city itself- the troll-mounted riders stood to the sides, two by two, probably to guard the flanks. It was then that they could see what Satan meany by air support. There, in the large, mostly ruined and cratered fields off to the left within the wall, was a strange and mighty host which could only be termed impressive. There were some hundreds of beings there that were best described as giant women, with giant wings, four arms, and holding a wild array of weapons- with one set of arms they carried what appeared to be pikes, but they had sacks on their backs that Dawn remarked looked a lot like her bag of fireballs. Satan advanced Charred sis to his vanguard- a troop of some dozens of heavily armored demons, taller and larger than the rest- rambling about magick in hopes that she "wouldn't get the rest of her face immolated when the fighting started."

The winged host took flight but they weren't alone in drifting around the rest of Satan's army in circles, slowly ascending- the ground off to the other side began to cave in and a swarm of new beings joined the strange aerial dance as well; they were bizarre and warped, like tree trunks with one eye right in the center, no apparent mouth, truncated roots below twisted into themselves, wings far too small to let them fly- Adam and Germaine simultaneously asked the Devil how they were flying when their wings weren't even moving. "They're like blimps and full of pestilent gas lighter than air" he remarked. This eerie assembly was strange indeed, and these were probably the most bizarre beings Germaine had seen thus far in the post-fungal world, and that was going some.

SICKNESS IN HELL

The last creature to emerge from the city was something neither he nor any other had spotted before- it was like a giant, about forty feet tall, and gleaming lightly like it was carved from solid rock. "A golem" Satan said. "I didn't have time to carve one out of wrought iron so I just laid out some rocks and animated them. Let's see that crazy old witch deal with this one!"

The golem hunched over the ground taking a step for every six steps any of the demons took while keeping up the distance. At intervals it roared various short phrases all involving death. "We will soak the soil in blood!" and "I will molest the corpses of our adversaries!" were heard frequently as the troop continued its advance. Its twisted face was admittedly grotesque, and while the demons frequently were dotted with specks of drool from their ever humid mouths, the golem was speckled with little splotches of chaffed rock which emerged as it spoke, ground to powder by its gigantic stone jaws.

The army literally parted ways at the bottom of the valley- most of the columns marched right through the dirt path Germaine had utilized previously when he had been scouting the area- the others marched double time along past the low slopes directly North and through a short stretch of forest to a service road which in turn led to about the same spot in Hillcrest on its East side where the main road began; this was not performed without difficulty, since the demons forced to depart the main force grumbled about less easy terrain.

It wasn't that long after the force reassembled and

took a very brief breather that they had marched halfway across Hillcrest and began to encounter resistance; the necromantic old woman had positioned a rather large host of creatures directly in their path; not zombies and skeletons as she had raised before, but strange beings which looked almost like they were formed out of taffy, their purple, pulsating limbs drawn out long from pale, languishing bodies- they had proboscises in place of mouths, and immediately rushed the front line when it emerged over the slight hill onto more level ground in the downtown region. More poured out of several businesses and homes along the road, endangering the flanks of the front column, which took up the entire road as the troll riders held back. Forming ranks, the demons allowed them to pile on them and smashed them with their shields, poking their pikes through and jabbing at them to drive them away, but some of them broke through and dragged a dozen or so of these Hellish denizens to the side of the road, where they buried their faces into their bodies, drawing out the blood and fluids from them with horrific screaming. Satan, unperturbed by this antagonistic assault, laughed and ordered that these unfortunate soldiers should be abandoned; and the column ignored the beings, which swarmed over the dying troop, marching past, wary to keep their shields up in case the distracted mosquito-zombies exhausted their prey and decided to attack again.

The next adversary they had to deal with, two blocks from the fortified church yard itself, was even stranger; the meat tree had apparently been enslaved and was rooted in the middle of the road right in their way, along with several apparent dwarven spawn, meat bushes, they might be termed, their knotted limbs braided with muscular tissues, dripping with various splotches of flesh which they had ripped off of some sort of life form and consumed some time before; they were more horrible than the tree, for while the latter had bark hiding its innards, these newer growths did not, and they could see the xylem and phloem running in streaks upwards on their woody flesh, pulsing like veins and arteries, carrying the toxic nutrients upwards and downwards in a frantic biological dance of death; Dawn wanted to burn the trees, but the fireball she tossed exploded against the side of one of the bushes and did virtually nothing, the photosynthetic freak ignoring the wall of fire that erupted in front of it, simply lifting its roots out of the road, dislodging several chunks of asphalt (which began to drip and melt from the heat) and moved backwards a few yards, planting itself again, refusing to move to the side out of the way. Its front, browned by the flames, folded inwards, undulating back into its own mutant flesh, emerging bright and new and apparently unaffected.

Satan commanded that his own tree-freaks should be the ones dealing with this distraction. Dozens of the gas-bloated, one eyed stumps that he had created soon dropped down from the swirling air force above, into the mass of meat bushes; the meat bushes attempted to whack the flying stump-mutants with their muscular arms, the flying stumps belched out clouds of noxious fumes which withered the flesh of the meat bushes, burning off their limbs. Not wanting any of his demons to have their own flesh melted away, Satan ordered the column to simply observe and do nothing.

SICKNESS IN HELL

After some minutes the path was no longer littered with meat bushes but rather the ashen, burned remnants of the same, although a few of the flying stumps had been pounded in half by the knotted flesh of the necromancers' plant soldiers; one of these unfortunate beings laid by the side of the road, having been smashed so hard it had been blasted into the side of a house and cracked the framing, spearing itself on the wood there and losing all of its gas. The deflated stump attempted to re-inflate itself, wheezing like a bellows pierced by a dagger as it repeatedly failed. Satan thought this was hilarious but Charred Sis must have taken pity on the plant and vampirized it entirely, to put it out of its misery, draining its life away until it was nothing more than a shriveled husk.

The meat tree fared better than its smaller counterparts and flailed its branches like they were ball and chain arrangements, whipping them around and forming a sort of shield out of its own limbs; the flying stumps were not able to close in and deliver their acrid fumes to it, and the breeze created by its arms would have deflected that too- it didn't help that what few leaves it possessed were as sharp as razors, and it sliced one of the stumps in half when it got a little too close, sending its lower half spinning into the front line of the army, leaking acidity which steamed and melted right into the asphalt below them.

With the evil tree distracted, though, Satan left behind some of the flying stumps to keep it busy and the army simply filed past it on either side of the road, several yards from its flailing limbs, slowing down their advance as it could only continue in two-by-twos, instead of a ten demon wide column; the troll riders were too large to perform this maneuver and had to use the next road over, marching through and smashing through debris scattered around in their way.

As soon as the front of the column emerged on the other side of the block past the meat tree, which was still waving its branches around behind the first segment of Satan's army, it came under attack by the front column of the necromancers' army. The zombies assembled there were not well armed, but they vastly outnumbered the demons, and it turned into a scene of carnage as the front ranks piled their shields together, simply lining up like a Roman formation, the mindless foes piling up and trying to get through to the flesh beyond this wall of iron- the troll riders also got bogged down in this manner; and though the zombies could not bite through the trolls' leathery, elephantine flesh, and although they were too stupid to climb the trolls to get at the riders, and although the riders peppered them with bolts and dropped them by the thousands, this was a most unwelcome spectacle, as the attackers, unless utterly dismembered, simply revived themselves after about thirty seconds and continued. Losses were slight on the Satanic side of the fray, but they didn't seem able to destroy the onslaught because of its enchanted nature. Dawn leaned over to Satan and suggested that they be purged by flame.

As he gazed at the death ahead of him, amused, Satan remarked that he had a better idea but that she could burn as many of them as she liked, and handed her several more bags of the little fire orbs she had been given before.

SICKNESS IN HELL

With a squeal of delight, like that of a school girl receiving a pony, she began tossing the little enchanted balls up over the front line, bringing down a regular barrage of flame which engulfed ten or more of the attackers at a time. Not hardened like the meat trees before, their bodies were consumed at great speed; their dry, desiccated faces were lit up like christmas trees and the fire burned their flesh off until there was nothing left but blackened, carbonized eye sockets, their bones flaming, these defleshed skeletons, with bits of burning meat falling off with displays of sparkles, dancing about blindly until their bones became too weak to contain their magic; when the skeletons began to crumble, with a snapping noise the enchantment was broken and a bit of bluish smoke exploded from their skulls.

Charred Sis had an idea too and clambered up into one of the homes next to the road, as Dawn, below, continued with great glee to burn everything in her path- she perched on the little corner porch which had been built there by some eccentric old person years ago and spread forth her hands, beginning to vampirize the attackers, severely draining their ability to move, rendering large numbers of them sluggish and some outright immobile. With their motions reduced, they could then be hacked apart so their magickal bodies would not reform themselves.

Satan was already working on the final solution.

"Germaine, quick, say horrible and nasty things to me."

SICKNESS IN HELL

"What?"

"I have to get off so I can break the magick, I need some stimulation."

"Uh, rancid snail meat? Burning flesh? Molested priests?"

Satan seemed to enjoy this general banter and reached down to fiddle with himself, his hand slipping under his miniskirt as his eyes rolled back a little. Germaine kept listing grotesque things for several minutes, and luridly described the carnage and suffering of Hell, in great detail, and this caused Satan to orgasm, his penis suddenly stretching out straight and wriggling around just like an earthworm, rocking back and forth- what came out was a flash of red energy which exploded outwards like a warhead blast, casting a massive shadow in every direction where the light was blocked by his troops, the flash literally disintegrating several hundred of the zombies before them, and apparently depriving the rest of their protection. With a post-orgasmic roar of adrenaline, he ordered a charge and the front line smashed its way through, rending the zombies limb from limb and tossing them out of their way, kicking the corpses, now unable to revive, aside. Germaine jogged ahead of the front and off to the side, and began experimenting with the bolt gun, spraying down those hordes unfortunate enough to be at a corner between the trolls on one street and the main column on the other, blasting off heads and arms and legs, leaving the dripping remnant behind as he walked through, waving the gun back and forth, until he had expended his bolts, reaching down to affix another of the little drums; he couldn't figure out how to reload the thing and retrieved the dagger on his belt instead and waded into the few that were still in his way, slashing them apart and pounding them with his left forearm after stabbing them with the blade, crushing their bones. The last zombie in his way was the most unfortunate of all, for he grabbed its mouth and wrenched its lower jaw to the side to crack it, then, as it struggled and tried to claw at him to get him off, he ripped its lower jaw off and left it standing there aghast, phlegm dripping from its exposed nasal openings, unable to bite, and in too much pain to move. With a kick to the back of its head he put it out of its suffering and rejoined the column.

The front of the attackers was now gone, and the last block was clear- soon the army assembled before the churchyard, where the necromancer had run a series of large wooden poles into the barrier around it and affixed a large amount of steel sheeting around the same, forming a barrier that was far larger than previously it had been. The old woman herself stepped out from the steps and mounted a sort of tower right beside the gate and leered out over the onlookers.

"You retarded people, I'm not going anywhere. Begone!"

She fired a bolt of energy out of her hands and Satan did the same at the same time; the two bolts exploded when they impacted one another, releasing an explosive ball of smoke which smelled of sulfur and wafted from this central point lazily on the light breeze off over the trolls and into the yards there.

"You begone wretch, give up your power, it's mine." Satan called for the valkyries to start their assault, and the same, by the hundreds flocked over the church yard and began dropping their fireballs, the same exploding all over the yard and ripping apart walls and roofs alike, engulfing the barracks altogether, and blasting the belltower so badly that it collapsed in seconds, falling inwards into the church itself, where a roar of fire burst through the windows, shattering them and sending shards of glass in every direction. Screeching about vandalism, the old woman began frantically summoning everything in the vicinity; corpses, trees, bushes, piles of rock, even the fence around the yard itself, which sprang to life- four of the wooden poles lifted themselves out of the earth and began stomping at the demons there, connected only by strands of magickal energy and a random jumble of trash for a body, which dangled on these same connective strands as it waddled and wavered and attempted and almost succeeded at stabilizing its horrendously vestigial form.

Satan wasn't dealing with this and sent a wall of lightning in its general direction, vaporizing it entirely, then took flight, landing on top of the church where the belltower once sat, standing there in the fire with his skirt uplifted by the hot air rising from the smoldering wooden wreckage below inside the shell of the building. He began randomly firing off spells at the old woman, and she did the same, as he roared to his forces to invade. The melee that erupted was perhaps even more chaotic than Hell, as the

SICKNESS IN HELL

demons and trolls hurried through the opening where the
necromancers' golem has been destroyed- Satan's own
golem was not far behind the back of the column, having
ripped the meat tree out of the road, and was now
brandishing it like a giant flail, roaring threats and insults
and attacking from the other side of the yard, kicking the
fence out of its way and hurling the thrashing tree into the
gate, where it got stuck in the wooden barrier, still
attacking anything in proximity with its branches and now
thrashing its roots in a similar manner.

The gigantic stone man didn't stop there though, and
began laughing as only a giant stone man can, a deep
rumble like the crack of a boulder tossed into a rocky
tunnel system, ripping off its own left hand and tossing it
towards the old woman, missing her but shattering the
wooden scaffolding underneath her. Unable to focus on the
golem and Satan at the same time, still hurling fire,
lightning, and other magick at the Devil, the floor below
her gave way, and she shrieked as she fell backwards into
the pile of rubble. Sensing victory, Satan swooped forth
from his perch directly on top of her, pounded her in the
head to knock her out, and commanded his vanguard to
form a wall around him, which they did with astonishing
speed, the more heavily armored demons forming a triple
rank to keep him from being distracted as he began to
siphon the force back out of the old crone.

With her magick decreasing by degrees, the
capabilities of her remaining forces did the same; the
zombies roving around the general vicinity at random
began to wear down, losing their cognitive skills, until they

were little more than hulking corpses with a weak force keeping them from falling apart altogether, unable to do more than twitch or crawl, or at best, to shuffle in one direction without the ability to change course, running up against walls or falling when their feet hit a pothole. The meat tree, finally free of its magickal bonds, righted itself and almost immediately buried itself back in the mushroom patch, sated with its condition. Haphazardly summoned entities of various shapes and sizes, engaged in combat with demons, and at first doing just fine by virtue of their force, now were overwhelmed and smashed apart by them, rent and stabbed, mutilated and burned, beaten and chopped apart.

Satan ended his siphoning, having largely expended the old broads' abilities, dismissed the vanguard, and gazed slowly around the yard about him, seeing the final victory of his army, and was pleased, smiling warmly. Gran walked up to him and offered him pie, having forced her way through a couple of zombie guards into the storage area almost as soon as the army broke through into the area.

"Delicious" he said, smashing two of them into his mouth at the same time.

When the necromancer came to, she was perhaps a bit more humble than she had been before. Deprived of most of her craft, what little magick remained only did so because Satan felt sorry for her for her insanity and admittedly admired her sadistic, twisted attitude. She couldn't fling fireballs around, but she could at least perform rudimentary acts involving telekinesis- Satan declared that now, for her crimes, her punishment was ten years of tributary servitude, and proclaimed that he'd keep her alive for this task and then see if her attitude adjustment was proper enough to allow her some leeway and some of her skills back. Charred Sis, already imparted the same power by the necromancer herself, and already skilled in her art, was allowed to keep the portion she had received with Satan's blessing; an admittedly smaller portion than the old woman had originally obtained, and a portion which Satan considered not to be a threat.

Despondent but unable to resist, the woman was led off by a troop of demons, which taunted her sporadically as they frog-marched her back to the city Satan had constructed, the troop accompanied by the flying stumps and valkyries, which were not needed to mop up any remnant force they might encounter. Adam suggested that the shambling zombies left behind might be good as a slave labor force- being mindless and only able to stagger around. He said they might be able to hook a few dozen of them to a gear system and use it to grind things to powder or something, or maybe just put them on leashes and keep them by the gate to frighten any attackers.

Turning to the mutants themselves, Satan apologized for the damage done to the yard- which was, building to building, variously either nothing but charred remains or little more than ruined shell. He would have them rebuilt better than before, he said, and invited them all to a victory celebration, which would take place in a few days back in his city; meanwhile, New Hell would be rebuilt. He promised them it would be a party for the ages.

CHAPTER XVIII: A NEW BEGINNING

The fateful night of the victory celebration, all of the family, sitting out in front of the Eastern wall of their enclosure watching a horde of goblins rebuild everything as best they could, stood in watch over the road waiting for Satan to arrive.

"I think he must have gotten drunk or something and forgot." Adam was pessimistic about the situation; but Germaine wasn't particularly worried; it's not like they couldn't just get some of the good stuff from their local demons and drink until they passed out if Satan failed to come through.

"What the hell is that?"

Germaine put a hand to his ear. Off in the distance somewhere in the sparse woods lining the outer ridge of Hillcrest, he could hear a little noise like chimes or something like that. A jingling sound.

"HO HO HO!"

With a roaring blast, several trees exploded out of the ground, root and all, not ten yards distant from them. Out from this gap in the greenery emerged two hideous creatures, and then two more, four pairs in all, hitched up to a gigantic sleigh made of a crudely painted, blood-smeared platform apparently carved out from a rail car. These creatures, bellowing and coughing up waves of sticky phlegm then sucking it back in like a cow mortifying its re-chewed cud, were as large as elephants, and disgustingly coated with loose hanging flesh that appeared to have at one time been bloated with decay- corpses, brought back to life; they noted that each one had a little jingle bell affixed to its neck by a ribbon. There, on the sleigh, was Satan in a full Santa Claus costume, flanked by several demons, and a merry looking, grinning Astaroth, covered in tinsel and holding several pine boughs like he was a Christmas Tree.

"Satan Claus is here to pick up all you naughty boys and girls for the big party. Maybe you can sit on Satan's lap and he'll give you a big, big gift." He laughed at his own joke, and hit one of the elephantine "reindeer" across the head with a chunk of white rock- compressed talcum perhaps judging by its powdery emittance- as though the same were a snowball.

"But it isn't even November yet." Gran was concerned about proper holiday schedules.

"Oh it isn't Christmas we're just doing what the christians did for so many centuries and stealing their holiday and moving the date. There's going to be a whole lot of fucking going on later, as is proper."

The "sleigh" contained many rows of seats, and although they were a bit uneven and cramped together (Peter decided to sit on a loose pile of burlap sacks instead of a seat and resembled a malevolent space worm holding court in the back) they all sat in their spaces and Satan wheeled his vehicle around, the necromantic elephants charging straight back into the woods, smashing up into small trees and plowing them over as they went, creating, it seemed, their own makeshift path over uneven surfaces by the combined weight of such a group of behemoths.

The city itself, they saw, had been expanded somewhat- the entire top of the mountain was now nothing more than a series of crenelated and roughly carved towers lining its entire front, extending back from that first peak and encompassing a second, which seemed to be connected to the first by several gleaming tunnels. Germaine asked what those were.

"Train tubes, we're building a railway for better movement of brimstone. We've dug out tunnels and shafts leading down into the foundations of the earth for some miles already. But we can discuss our progress later, we have some drugs to do."

He waved his hand and started materializing little green bags in the same, his other hand holding the reins and guiding his corpse steeds up the path towards the entrance to the mountains. He passed these out like candy- marijuana, and then cocaine and various pills also. A few of them weren't much interested in narcotics, but Adam mumbled something about the war and snorted enough blow to lay low a seasoned mack daddy.

Upon entering the massive front hall, where the lungshrimp pool had been covered over with a series of wooden walkways- decorative and sturdy it seemed- in Satan's words "so that we can see it without falling in it," they were received by a large gaggle of Satan's flying troops- those nubile Valkyries which were now covered in oil and began making vague sexual remarks at all of them the moment they arrived. Satan told them to go away for a bit, they could come to the party too but the special guests had to be shown the 'room' first.

The 'room' turned out to be a gigantic inner hall- it was at least a quarter mile long, and almost as wide, with one giant pillar right in the center and enormous arches angling upwards and curving down the sides of the room in ridges, some several hundred feet above- an impressive sight, which was almost entirely coated in some sort of sparkly material.

"Herkimer diamonds" Satan told them all. "They're nice and glittery. And those up there, "he pointed to a dozen or so spots of glowing light among the arches, at the center of each ridge, "are little bits of luminescent magical force. They can even change color." He snapped his fingers and the soft yellow glow became an intense white light, bright as the sun and glancing off every surface, until it seemed they were in a cheap 80s era fantasy movie. With another snap of his fingers they began shifting size melted into a sort of luminescent cloud which drifted around the vaulted ceiling with a low bluish light, tendrils of the same dancing lazily around the room, falling to their very level and sweeping the floor itself, apparently non reactive to breeze or perturbation by touch. These tendrils of glowing light, gentle and wondrous, ebbed around the room like dimly lit pillars.

SICKNESS IN HELL

"Amazing" Dawn said, marveling at this strange spectacle.

"Gimme a minute to change." Satan Claus jogged off into a side room and slammed the door behind him, waving his hands like he had become temporarily retarded, making strange noises for his own amusement. Astaroth, still dressed like a Christmas Tree, was left to his own devices and huddled up next to the central pillar, laughing under his breath and shaking and spasming with glee.

It didn't take more than two minutes for Satan to return, and now he had emerged as the ultimate pimp daddy of all time; he had on a purple suit, with a fuzzy cane and everything, a pair of fuzzy dice dangling from a purple tophat upon his wrinkled forehead, already grooving his way across the floor; he didn't have any pants on and his penis was grooving just like the rest of him.

"Now, it's party time!"

With a snap of his fingers a set of lights on all sides of the room angling up at the walls shot to life, casting slowly flashing, changing colors at them, as the walls themselves folded back and upwards away from the room into many hollow spaces which had been behind them the whole time. Within was a regular horde of life- demons, valkyries, trolls and goblins, hobgoblins and ogres, banshees and ghouls and succubi and vampires, werewolves and monsters of every description, mostly mutilated, all of them beginning to dance as a low hum emitted from the walls themselves grew into a sort of throbbing beat, which quickly was replaced by a disco groove- not the foolish and meaningless disco of the United States as its original sound was displaced by a bunch of Scandinavians that didn't know what they were doing, but the good shit- disco from Spain and Italy and places like that, where people were too busy in its heyday doing drugs to add a melody to the pounding synth and obviously mechanized drumming.

A huge table came out of the ceiling, still studded with shining quartzite crust- this gleaming fixture was topped with every food and drink imaginable, and it settled in along the walls, little stairways in between each section of table fusing seamlessly with the hollows which had been revealed in the walls themselves prior- this allowed the grotesque assembly beyond to groove its way down into the party floor, which too began to change; as Adam very quickly stumbled through a line of gorgons to gorge himself on any food he thought tasty looking, most of them stood there in shock; the floor, once a flat surface of stone, flashed with green light and then settled down to a dim glow, now comprised of a massive number of squares of light, each now changing on its own accord in random tandem with the beat, green and blue and red and yellow, white and even, somehow, black- the shadowy glow casting shadow in lieu of light.

The demonic disco persisted as the entire assembly began feasting and dancing and making merry. Dawn was already thronging among them, apparently desiring to go chat up the valkyries and ask them what Hell was really like. Peter looked like he wanted to kill himself though, since his deformity made it impossible to dance.

"I feel your pain" said Astaroth, unable to groove effectively while pretending to be a tree. "You might try the flip flop, though, I hear it's all the rage at parties involving politicians."

He didn't have to feel so lonely after all though, since Satan had apparently created some sort of worm-demon hybrid at some point and they shared his general shape and form. With a now happy Peter in the lead, they formed a line and wiggled along the floor, flopping up and down and propelling themselves at the same time with their arms. A few hobgoblins, moving too slowly to avoid this line, were crushed into the floor, getting up as the line of increasingly drunk revelers worked past them and fleeing towards the buffet tables.

Satan, in his element, almost immediately began humping one of his valkyries, levitating up in the air and grooving across the air under the arches while she was wrapped around him wings and all, thrusting against his body. This seemed to please him, and Astaroth looked longingly upon the same group of winged, nude women who were still dancing or standing to the sides laughing and drinking and eating their dinner. After a moment he tossed the tree boughs away and went off to see if he could get lucky in love.

It turned out that a fairly large proportion of demons were homosexual. There were other random sex acts being performed sporadically about the hall in full view of everyone else around them; lesbian valkyries, making out and knocking food off the tables, demons truncating one anothers' colons on a random basis, Dawn getting flashed by a curious troll which revealed, much to her displeasure, his mastodonic manhood to her; she ran the other way, laughing at the spectacle, leaving the troll apparently embarrassed but too drunk to react properly.

"TEA TIME!"

Satan shouted down to them all and was now, instantaneously, wearing a pink dress instead of a disco suit. Every sex act was terminated instantly, every dance ended. He slowly levitated down to the floor, and the tables, which had been covered in literal acres of food, were now cleared by his magic and replaced with silver platters of crumpets and croissants and cookies, paired with enormous pots of tea the size of kegs- there was chamomile, mint tea, black and orange cut tea, green tea, and tea from mushrooms.

Silently, the demons and other Hell spawn began filing to the walls to retrieve this treat, then sat down in groups sipping the hot tea with their pinky fingers (if they had any fingers) extended. Germaine and company followed suit, not bothering to ask what this strange ritual actually was. Adam, who had railed enough cocaine earlier to kill the average human, was extremely happy because his throat was dry from all the marijuana he kept smoking to level out his constitution.

Only ten minutes passed, the music changing from a

heavy disco beat to the light plunking of a revolution-era fortepiano, accompanied by harp overtones.

"Okay enough of that gay stuff."

Satan waved his hand again and hurled his tea cup into the crowd then started shaking and went temporarily insane, roaring and physically assaulting several demons which had sat down to take their tea beside him; the disco beat returned and he calmed down but was still in the pink dress he had been wearing prior, forgetting to change back into his disco suit. Nobody thought it wise to tell him. The food and drink, at least, was magically changed on its various tables, back to something more substantial than tea and tea accessories.

The party continued for nobody knew how long. By the end of the night almost everyone was inebriated and many were presumably pregnant from sexual acts- if, indeed, Germane surmised, it was possible for the spawn of Hell to become impregnated. Amusingly a couple of the children should any be born were probably Adams, since in his coke frenzy he was willfully interacting with any being that showed interest. Gran was showing her true flower child nature also, but turned out to be far more interested in fellatio than penetration, as she displayed for them all to see when she was unable to get a troll phallus inside and had to borrow a knife from one of the demons to get her cheeks cut open a little.

Germaine was honestly considering incest with his sister more than anything else, but he was too drunk to do anything and decided in a moment of startling brilliance to wait until he was actually sober and in command of his faculties. It didn't help the temptation that she ended up sprawled out across his lap with half her ass showing because there was no other comfortable spot to pass out in.

"I would like to make a short announcement if I may."

Satan waved his hands again and the music became far more quiet, just a faint echo along the pillar, which was vibrating slightly with the beat, as though it too wished to dance a bit. The general laughter and chatting also quieted down but never ceased.

"While we've been partying here your entire town has been improved substantially." He pointed in the general direction of the mutant family there, half of them passed out in puddles of vomit from too much demonic liquor. "I wanted you here so we could get the work done faster and so it would be a surprise. Since it isn't done yet you should all stay here for a sleepover tonight. Half of you are asleep anyways." He glanced sideways at Gran, who was so drunk she was muttering to herself, half asleep, apparently arguing with an imaginary friend about baking pies.

Germaine was worried that "sleepover" meant "come do gay things with me in my chamber" but the offer was never made. Perhaps Satan knew he wasn't interested in such a thing, or maybe he was sated from fucking his valkyries for the last ten hours or so.

SICKNESS IN HELL

"Don't worry everyone, half of you will be hung over tomorrow but you can always get some hair of the dog for that."

With one final wave of his hand Satan caused the lights to flash one last time then settle back into being the same stone floor as prior. The lights along the walls dimmed and the crowd generally began to file (or rather stumble) through to various exits which led off in many directions to parts of the city. It seemed this city lacked any significant order though because many remained, still eating, chatting, or doing whatever else they desired. As Germaine carried Dawn on his back, still dripping with a bit of vomit, through one of the exits, intent on exploring a bit and maybe checking out the railway Satan had mentioned, accompanied by Zak and coked up Adam, who was twitching and muttering, he saw that some of these spawn had already resumed various bits of work they apparently desired to accomplish- a couple of trolls with clubs were smashing away at a wall not ten yards outside the hall, as a few demons took turns dumping buckets of the same debris, swept up, over the side of the city a couple of hallways away. The halls were full of demons, some working, some chatting, some drunkenly staggering, others asleep.

They ended up sleeping in one of those same halls as a group of demons looked on, chatting in the dim light for hours until the sunrise. Each one of them was at complete ease surrounded by the power of the Devil.

THE END

CPSIA information can be obtained
at www.ICGtesting.com
Printed in the USA
LVOW10s2153030617
536844LV00011B/845/P